BRIDPORT PRIZE 2024

EXTRACTS FROM THE NOV

JUDGE
Ross Raisin

redcliffe

First published in 2024 by Redcliffe Press Ltd

e: info@redcliffepress.co.uk
www.redcliffepress.co.uk
Follow us on X @RedcliffePress

Follow The Bridport Prize:
Follow us on X and Instagram @BridportPrize
www.bridportprize.org.uk
www.facebook.com/bridportprize

ISBN 978-1-915670-19-9

British Library Cataloguing-in-Publication Data
A catalogue record for this book is available from the British Library

Typeset in 10.5pt Times

Typeset by Addison Print Ltd, Northampton
Printed by Hobbs the Printers Ltd, Totton

MIX
Paper | Supporting responsible forestry
FSC® C020438
www.fsc.org

WORLD LAND TRUST™
www.carbonbalancedprint.com
CBP2250

Contents

Turn your own page

Words matter, more than ever. The stories we tell each other bring us together. Whether it's turning the page or turning up the volume of an audiobook, writers make a difference in our everyday lives. They cause us to laugh, cry, discover, wonder. Novels create a world where we can forget our own predicament or understand it better. Some novels never leave us.

Writing a novel is a hard fought journey. Climbing a mountain of words with the inevitable twists, turns and disappointments takes courage. However, there are also moments of breathtaking joy. Walking into a bookshop or seeing your novel online in all its completed glory is a truly unforgettable, life defining moment.

The writers in this anthology found the time and energy to craft their novels. How? Whether for ten minutes or two hours, their creativity became a priority. Slowly but surely things took shape. Yes there were times of intense frustration, endless editing and re-writing but just look what they achieved.

Our patron, best selling author and former Bridport Prize winner, Kit de Waal knows only too well 'how prizes can change your writing life.'

It starts here.

Congratulations everyone. Thank you for trusting us with your words. Keep writing!

The Bridport Prize Team

Where are they now?
Our fab five former winners

Chetna Maroo
Western Lane was shortlisted for the 2023 Booker Prize, longlisted for the Women's Prize for fiction 2024 and William Hill Sports Book of the Year 2023.

Megan Davies
The Messenger was shortlisted for the CrimeFest Specsavers Debut Crime Novel Award 2024. *Bay of Thieves* was a *Sunday Times* book pick of the month.

Lara Haworth
Monumenta 'fizzes with ideas' says *The Guardian* review. 'The Bridport Prize changed my life,' says Lara.

Elaine Chiew
The Light Between Us was a BBC Open Book summer read recommend.

Rowe Irvin
Life Cycle of a Moth was part of a five way auction and is set for publication in 2025.

Novel Award Partners

The Bridport Prize is proud to work in partnership with the following organisations in the delivery of the Peggy Chapman-Andrews Award for a First Novel.

A.M. Heath Literary Agents

Founded in 1919 by Audrey Heath and Alice May Spinks, two women who challenged the conventions of publishing, we are a London literary agency still very much driven by a passion to help writers who want to shift, shape or enrich the wider cultural conversation, and provide irresistible entertainment.

Championing our clients' writing remains at the heart of what we do. As well as a century of experience, we bring energy, ambition, and a keen eye for detail to our work.

We're always looking out for original ideas combined with great quality writing, and we work with the Bridport Prize to encourage emerging writers. By helping to draw up the long-list and short-list for the Peggy Chapman-Andrews Award for a First Novel, we aim to support the best new novelists to find publishers and readers across the world.

Website: www.amheath.com
X: @EuanThorneycrof / @AMHeathLtd

Headline Fiction

Headline Fiction publishes the novels people really want to read; the books that keep them reading into the early hours, with worlds people want to escape to and with characters they can relate to. We pride ourselves on understanding readers, what drives them to buy and read books and where and how they read them. Our reach is broad, encompassing literary and commercial imprints and some of the best (and bestselling) storytellers in the business. We publish books that win prizes, top charts and reach millions of readers around the world.

Website: www.headline.co.uk
X: @headlinepg
https://www.facebook.com/headlinebooks/

The Literary Consultancy

The Literary Consultancy is the UK's first and leading writing consultancy, offering editorial services since 1996. Its aim is to provide honest, professional feedback to writers to give them a better sense of whether and where their work might fit into the ever-changing market.

TLC and its team of world-class professional editors work with writers writing in English at all levels, across all genres. Its most popular services include manuscript assessment, developmental editing, submission package reports, and one-to-one mentoring. It is also home to Being A Writer, a membership platform for writers who want to create happier, healthier writing habits.

TLC meets writers on the page. Its services and resources equip writers with the context, confidence, and skills they need to thrive and flourish.

Email: info@literaryconsultancy.co.uk
Website: literaryconsultancy.co.uk
X: @TLCUK
Facebook: The Literary Consultancy

ROSS RAISIN

Judge's Report

From the very first line, the sentence-by-sentence flow of this year's winner, *The Legatees*, is electric. This is a novel that courses with vulnerability and humour, mischief and sorrow, as we follow its narrator, Joyce, through the early, numbed progress of grieving for her lover – a celebrated artist whom we come to understand groomed her from a much younger age. It is through sophisticated storytelling, though, not salaciousness, that we become drawn into her world: through subtle shifts in the atmosphere; descriptions that spear the particularity of a moment; interactions that are by turns mortifying and very funny.

All of the relationships in *The Legatees* are drawn with nuance and originality. I love that the novel never does the obvious thing. The characters are always behaving like themselves – never like characters I recognise from other books; behaving always (to borrow one of my well-worn teaching catchphrases) with plausible surprise – whether in the decision to escape from a dinner party, or in a smaller action such as Joyce studying a doodle that someone has made of her and judging the actions of her cartoon self.

That dinner party scene is worth another mention, because it is fantastic. A cake-slice of art-world social awkwardness, in its depiction of scenester pretention and desperation, a place where people behave with 'brisk professionalism masquerading as bonhomie'.

This is, in one sense, a novel about art, and the curation of legacy, the manipulative sleight of an artist's hand. But, moreover, it is a novel about a woman in limbo, searching, as she attempts to set straight the account of her deceased lover, for an agency in her own life that circumstance, and the control of others, have until now held from her.

It is no easy thing to write a child's voice that feels both original and believable – which is what the runner-up, *This is About an Alligator and Nothing Else*, manages to do. And I don't imagine it will surprise you to learn that the novel is, in fact, about more than an alligator. It is about a snake too, for one thing (and that's a scene which I am not going to forget in a hurry). It is also, minutely and engagingly, about Florida: a 'place shaped like a gun'; a place of sticky heat and themed birthday bibles and chunky chili powder home fries.

And also, with effective background menace, about corporate malevolence. A buddy novel to the backdrop of a giant sugar company, which offers bribes to the locals to not talk about all their doctor appointments; a community whose little children chat over their school lunch about all the loved-ones they have lost to big business.

Part vivid family drama about coming of age in the 90s, part literary ghost story, *Babygirl* is about May, a young woman who is left to bring up her niece following the death of her sister. Haunting, intimate and sharply observed, the novel explores themes of motherhood, female survival, and what is inherited and lost across four generations of a family of women.

Bound in Shallows offers a view of a future in which the land has been taken over by sea and salt. On a boat, a couple's intimate relationship is disrupted by the arrival of a man who threatens the balance of their dynamic, and by a sudden pregnancy. Deftly drawn, with characters we root for and want to survive, the author of this manuscript elegantly sets up a dystopia where the wind carries hope, and we will the characters forwards, into and through the dangers around them.

The River is a Brown God brilliantly evokes 1830s Texas, when Americans were the illegal aliens, flooding over the Sabine River into the Mexican Republic. This is a novel which also knows exactly what story it wants to tell and is able to impressively keep its focus as it develops. All the judges were impressed by the author's ability to create a setting which is both vivid and visceral, as well as conjuring up a piece of history which feels authentic and alive. There's a cinematic quality to the scene-setting which draws us in as readers, right from the first sentence. An impressive piece of work.

FIRST PRIZE

LAURA ALLSOP

The Legatees

Synopsis

The Legatees *is a novel exploring the slippages that occur between official and unofficial biographies – between the accepted narrative of a celebrated person's life and the messier, unvarnished reality. The story entwines three individuals' claims to the legacy of a revered but reclusive American painter named Jim Schiure following his suicide. Set in New York in 2008, the novel is narrated by Joyce, a woman in her late 30s who has been Jim's partner for 22 years, but whose existence is unknown to his circle and to the public. Through her narration, we learn that Joyce was groomed by Jim when she was still was a teenager and he was a successful, married artist in his 30s. Having lived her adult life largely in the shadows, prey to the whims of her difficult, mercurial partner, she finds herself exposed just before his death to Andrew, a longstanding friend of Jim's cherry-picked to write his biography. In possession of the unauthorised account, and desiring to know the other dimensions of her controlling and secretive partner, Joyce enters into a tentative friendship with Andrew, using her privileged position as Jim's lover to gain access to a world to which she has long been denied – all the time hiding the true nature of the relationship and, by extension, herself. She is simultaneously drawn into the acquaintance of a dilettante artist and collector of Jim's work whom he had been cultivating through written correspondence before his death. Discussing voice and its different deployments – in fiction, criticism, memoir and biography; as well as letters, interviews and the first-person essay form espoused by mostly young women in the last 15 years –* The Legatees *looks at the attempt to regain authorial agency by a woman schooled through a destructive relationship in manipulation.*

Chapter One

I wake up with a gasp, tearing through the last moments of sleep. This is the fourth night in a row that she's come for me.

He has already left the bed. The window is open, a small sign of his presence, even care, though the gesture is pointless: still curtains telegraph another flat, close day. I go downstairs, back to last night's scene. Flies are busying themselves over the remains of our dinner, the wilted leaves coated in vinegar, the grey meat edged with hard, white fat. I go to the sink for some water but find it full, the counter as dirty as the table. Cupping my right hand under the faucet, I bring water to my mouth, splashing the front of my borrowed cotton nightdress, making the thin pink material stick to my body like a second skin.

Outside is as slow and airless as in but I push open the doors anyway and walk through tangled grass as far as the gate. Once there, I throw a practised glance behind me, then let the usual handful of seconds pass before pushing on. The ground is cool and damp beneath my bare feet, the air around me a moving veil of insects.

Twenty-two years ago, when I was a child and stupid, he showed me a tiny sculpture from his collection. A pinkish female form in clay, lying on a dinky toy bed under a light pink net, eyes closed and mouth open, slack. It was small enough to pocket, so I did. By the time I time I gave it back, I had more or less become the little figure, or maybe it was more accurate to say that the little figure was now me: my mouth wearied into pliancy, my gaze well shut.

I'm about five hundred yards from his house when it starts to rain, fat drops hitting my face like spittle. I'm back within minutes to an unchanged kitchen, the door open as I left it. A wasted protest. I wipe my face, move the remains of dinner to one side and write longhand on a legal pad in short, unproductive stints as the rain comes in sideways through the door. Bored, I give up and prowl around the house, taking care to avoid the hallway near his studio, moving in and out of the rooms, opening windows and drawers, fingering the same photographs and tchotchkes I have scrutinised and palpated for decades, scavenging for something new. Back in his bedroom, I curl up on the unmade bed, like a damp, slovenly cat.

Hours later, my nerves thin and blood surging, I am back in the kitchen. It's chilly now and there are puddles by the door where the rain's collected. Low-hanging black clouds menace the treetops. I imagine a fire blazing just beyond the horizon, somehow tearing through the mulch and canopy, threatening to eat us, this house, his work. Birds chatter and shriek. The eaves drip.

There's a click behind me, a lightbulb switched on.

"Strange hawk," he says.

* * *

"I hate this place," I tell him, after he's cleaned up the kitchen and begun preparing dinner.

"I know." He whistles a tune I don't recognise as he fillets a piece of fish. I light a cigarette, feeling unbuttoned, coquettish.

"It's a big pile of kindling. It could go up like that," I say, swapping the cigarette to my left hand and clicking my right fingers to demonstrate.

"Is that a threat?" he says.

"The damp might save you."

"Did you do any work today?"

"Tried."

"Too busy fantasising about a conflagration. When I die, you can burn the place down." He slaps the fish into a panful of hot oil, where it sizzles noisily. The room fills with a rancid, briny smell.

"They do that with trauma victims, you know," I say, once the pan has calmed. "Tear apart the place they were abused, burn it down. It's therapeutic." I flick my cigarette out into the wet grass. He leans back against the counter and lifts a hand to his mouth, too late to catch the yawn. Bringing it down, his elbow peeps through a hole in his sweater like a fleeting insult.

"Are you eating?" he asks.

I shake my head.

He reaches a hand to my face to push away the unruly strands that have fallen into my sightline. I glance up, but it is hard to look him in the eyes, even though they've recently started to water and blanche; even if, when he does smile, the creases in the skin around them are more and more deeply etched.

"Strange hawk," he says, tapping me on my beak. Then, more imperiously: "Sit down and eat."

"I don't like fish."

His laugh is a short, sharp exhalation. "We have fun, don't we?"

I let my mouth make the smile it wants to and sit down. He puts out plates, drops a little bundle of cutlery on the table and goes back for water.

"Did you get anything done today?" I ask, as his back is turned.

"Not much. But I sat and thought, which is as important. Your problem is your lack of discipline."

"I can't think if I'm tired. And I can't think anything coherent in this house." I push away the chipped enamel plate in front of me.

"Come on, eat something," he says, bringing over the fish, some bread and vegetables. "Don't be a bore."

"I'm not being a bore. And I'm not hungry," I say, tearing up a piece of bread into confetti.

He shrugs and starts on his dinner. He proceeds with absurd care, methodically cutting a piece from each type of food on his plate and layering the pieces one by one onto his fork in a series of neat little stacks. His mouth is pursed as he chews. Like this, he reminds me of my father.

"It's good," he tries again. I sigh noisily.

"You're looking much too thin," he says, irritation creeping back into his voice. "Don't you feed yourself in the city?"

"I'm the same as always. I don't feel hungry." There's another involuntary pull at the sides of my mouth as I hunch down further in my seat.

"You've been looking at the photos," he says. "I went to find one and the box had been ransacked."

"Aren't you always telling me to make myself at home?"

A series of loud, insistent knocks at the front door clips our fledgling argument.

We sit quietly, unconcerned, playing out our routine for the rare occasion someone turns up at the door. Two minutes pass, then three, then four, the time measured out in calm, indifferent increments by the fiercely tapered hands on the kitchen clock. He continues to eat until his plate is almost finished.

"Jim!" shouts a voice from behind the door. There's a brief pause before the banging resumes. "*Jim*!"

He drops his fork onto his plate and thinks for a moment. "It's Andrew."

Emboldened by the strangeness of the fact, I tell him: "I'm not hiding."

He pushes his grey hair up into a fleeting pompadour, and looks me over, taking in with fresh, critical eyes the stained nightdress I've been wearing all day, my unbrushed hair and bare face.

"I'll get dressed," I offer.

He nods. The banging starts up again.

"I'm coming!"

I'm impressed at the ease with which he is able to retune. It wouldn't occur to anyone hearing that delicately rumbled voice that its owner might not appreciate being disturbed so late at his house – situated, after all, miles from anywhere – with a decades-younger mistress sitting at the table, wearing his dead wife's nightdress.

I'm upstairs when he opens the door, taking off the ridiculous pink prairie confection I can't imagine anyone seriously wearing, even to bed, even twenty years ago, and wriggle into the jeans and sweater I wore when I first arrived. They're still in the hallway, but I can hear Andrew's voice getting louder, venturing further and further into the house. In the mirror, no longer a savage sprite in borrowed clothes, I try to see myself as a stranger, someone older, might: a woman in her early-to-mid-thirties, skin pale but unlined, body unadorned and offering no coordinates in terms of style or character – except, perhaps, the fact of being braless. I crack a minuscule smile and tiptoe back into the kitchen to reoccupy my seat. A current zips through me as I wait for them.

Andrew comes in first, walking backwards and facing Jim.

"I tried calling, but then I remembered your phone's never on," he is saying. Beneath the damp, leathery air he's ushered in with him, I can smell the booze evaporating from his pores. Just as he's turning around, he says, probably for the fifth time, "I hope I'm not disturbing you." When he sees me, his face is a cliché of a blank. I smile. He turns to Jim for clarification, but instead Jim points to a chair. Obediently, Andrew takes a seat.

"Some wine?" Jim asks.

Andrew nods and looks from Jim to me and back again.

"This is Joyce," Jim adds, as he fetches another glass.

"Hi," I say.

He greets me with a puzzled smile, as if he's waiting for a punchline. A tall, gangly figure with speckled grey hair, he's younger than Jim, maybe ten years, though his obsequiousness makes it seem like more. I suspend judgement; it is, after all, a quality of Jim's to make others immediately, acceptingly inferior.

Jim pours him a glass of wine and sits at the table across from him. "So: what's the matter?"

Andrew laughs, and shakes his head.

"This is going to sound so stupid," he starts.

"Come on," Jim says.

Andrew sighs, as if he's unsure, but the sigh is transparently rehearsed. "I've been worried about you." He pauses, leaving room for Jim to say something. The moment ticks past. "I was rereading our transcripts yesterday and I realised I hadn't seen or spoken to you in almost three months. I tried calling but couldn't get through. It got to this evening, and I felt desperate enough or drunk enough and I thought – why don't I just come here and see if you're OK? So I had a couple more drinks, got on the train and here I am." He delivers this last piece of information with a sheepish laugh.

Jim smiles. "You thought I'd slipped in the shower."

Andrew's laugh in response is a shade too enthusiastic. "I don't really know what I was thinking."

"Don't be sorry. You're right, it has been a while. I ought to have been in touch."

"Honestly, it's enough to know you're OK."

"That's kind of you. But I've been in the teeth of some new work. I'll show some of it to you, if you want."

At this, Andrew seems to bloom. "I would love that."

"I'll let Rodhri know to book you in. I've given him the summer off but he'll be back up here soon enough."

Ignoring Andrew's slightly strained smile, Jim continues, "Do you want dinner? There's plenty. Joyce isn't eating, for some reason."

We're both surprised to hear him speak my name. I shrug. Andrew blinks, says yes, he would love some food.

He eats his meal – what would have been my portion if I'd been hungry – enthusiastically, proclaiming it delicious, telling Jim what a wonderful cook he is. Jim accepts the compliments, pours more wine. I sip from my glass as they swap anecdotes, Andrew's much longer. He tells Jim about his last few months, about Venice, Kassel and Muenster, the wet European summer and persistent talk of climate change among the globetrotting art-folk. "The irony was totally unacknowledged," Andrew says, with a dry laugh. I picture him leaning over the railings of some yacht, marshy, petrol-scented air gusting up from green Venetian waters, and earnestly holding forth on the state of the ice caps. Jim smiles, interjecting here and there, but lets Andrew talk, which he does, happily, but every now and then I feel a tiny portion of his gaze and attention on me.

Another bottle of wine is opened, and drunk almost to the dregs before Andrew says, "I had another reason for coming."

"Oh?"

"It's twenty years. Isn't it? Twenty years today since she died. God, you must miss her."

There's a churn in the air as their interpersonal weather vane swings round. I've underestimated Andrew. I look at Jim and see the slight start, the slip of the mask.

He smiles evenly. "You're right. It is twenty years."

I watch, exhilarated, as Andrew reaches a hand across the table to grasp Jim's forearm.

"I miss her too," Andrew continues, then: "I found this the other day." He pulls a photograph from his pocket. It's small, with serrated edges, the image various shades of brown. I've hardly caught a glimpse before it's pressed into Jim's hands. He looks it over, his gaze dim and unreadable.

"We took it that day in Meridian, do you remember?" Andrew says.

Jim keeps his eyes on the image, signalling his assent with a slight shift. Andrew leans forward, blocking me out. "I have such a strong memory of that night. The three of us all tangled up in the back of the car, drunk as skunks."

There is a pause before Jim decides to speak: "I remember."

If Andrew hears the warning in Jim's voice, he does not heed it. With astounding presumption, he plucks the picture out of Jim's fingers, and looks at it. "She was so *vital*."

"Yes," Jim says, before taking a short, conclusive breath. "Well. It's been a long day. Joyce, would you mind making up the bed in the guest room?"

Silence.

"Sure."

Jim gets up and claps a hand on Andrew's shoulder. "I'm glad you came," he says, his voice starting to fill out again. "You sleep well, alright?"

He leaves the room and Andrew looks at me properly for the first time since arriving. Before he can say a word, I'm up and moving to the door. He follows me out along the dark hallway into the house, past the studio, with its emphatically closed door, and on to the guest bedroom. I hit the light-switch and squint as the energy-saving bulb flickers to life. Under its stuttering light, Andrew's expression is fractured into a sequence of stages, the face of a stranger in a night club in a dream.

"What just happened?" he says, ashen under the now-resolved white light.

ALEX CASSIDY

Mammoth

Synopsis

For chef Isa Maldona, the pursuit of creative independence and a Michelin star entangles her in a web of culinary obsession and scientific horror.

Isa Maldona is the executive chef of the Belgrano in London. Over a decade, she has helped them win a Michelin star and numerous awards. However, the restaurant is considered the brainchild of her mentor, Chef Timo Martinez. Long interested in starting her own restaurant, Isa has faced disappointment with false promises and failed projects. When an email arrives from the mysterious Primagen Industries seeking an executive chef to create a new restaurant, she sees it as an opportunity for independence.

At the interview, Isa discovers Primagen's secret: their patented mammoth tenderloin, bioengineered from fossils. Tasked with achieving a Michelin star within a year, she accepts despite some ethical objections. Assembling a team, including Ange, a former colleague and old flame, she dives into every element of the creative process. The relentless corporate pressure and pursuit of perfection lead her to isolate herself, spiralling into obsessive depression and revisiting memories of her parents, which conflict with her current reality. Her distance frustrates Ange, Timo, and her team.

Upon launch, the restaurant is a success. However, the secrecy behind Primagen causes issues with journalists and quality judges. Protests and media scrutiny arise, and Isa is grilled on television about her parent company. Isa demands clarity from Primagen and discovers they are cloning live mammoths and humans, including her employees, as spies.

Terrified, Isa seeks refuge with Ange. But she suspects Ange has been replaced by a Primagen clone. Fearing the consequences of her involvement, she vows to expose the truth, only to find Primagen has replaced her too. The book ends with her realisation that the restaurant will continue with her clone in charge.

Part 1
I took the email with a heap of salt:

Subject: Executive Chef Interview
Dear Chef Isa Maldona,
We hope this message finds you well. We are writing to inform you of an upcoming culinary venture that is poised to make huge waves in the world of global gastronomy.

As well as your experience, you have been selected on recommendation of another interviewee, Ange Powell, who we understand you previously worked with in your current capacity at The Belgrano.

As such, we invite you to an in-person interview for an Executive Chef position at a yet-to-be-launched establishment in London.

The interview will be an opportunity for us to explore your culinary background and vision, particularly your thoughts on speculative gastronomy. We will only need a few hours of your time. There is no need to bring anything but your insights and aspirations.

Timings for the interview are as follows:
Date: 04/07/2018
Time: 10:00am
Location: 3 South Place, London EC2M 2AF

We look forward to the possibility of meeting with you and discussing your potential role in guiding our exciting journey.

Sincerely,
The Growth & Marketing Team
Primagen Industries

There was no name for the restaurant, no name for the sender, and when I punched the address in on Google Maps it was an office block for a research company, not a kitchen.

They had used the right restaurant-opening-buzzwords though. All of these conversations *started off* exciting. I'd had dozens. The restaurant scene in London was always being shaken up and twisted round and disrupted, and by the time they were done, the things they were shaking up and twisting and disrupting were back in fashion anyway. There were always 'outside investors looking to make big waves'. Waves which broke long before they saw the shore.

As jaded as I was, I didn't disregard it completely because of Ange. They definitely wouldn't waste my time by suggesting me, which meant there was something substantial there.

But when I texted them about it, they were uncharacteristically cagey:

Ange

Yes! I knew they'd get in touch.

I know this is going to sound weird but I can't actually say anything about it atm, but please please please take the interview. We'll talk after. x

Equal parts intrigued and confused, I accepted the interview then put it out of my mind, which wasn't too hard to do.

One of the benefits of interviewing when you already have a job is you're too busy to worry.

I'd led the team as chef de cuisine at The Belgrano for nearly a decade. The restaurant, and, by extension, me, I was regularly named as one of the top female chefs in the capital, had a fantastic reputation. We'd been awarded multiple AA rosettes, ranked highly at the Restaurant Awards every year, earned our first Michelin star in 2015, and retained it in the three years since. We were fully booked until Christmas, and ran extra covers in the summer, our most important time.

Our food was at its best when London's evenings were at their longest. That special period when every corner becomes a beer garden and every person in the city seems to smoke. The parks spill over with sunbathers and each stone step and ledge becomes an impromptu table setting casting long shadows on narrow streets.

Londoners make the most of summer, because they know it doesn't last very long.

In that brief suntrap the kitchens and bars that fuel the city are at their hottest. The Belgrano was no different. By July we had settled into our summer rhythm where being busy felt better than standing still.

I managed a team of 30 kitchen staff and 20 front-of-house. They were stellar. All trained in top kitchens or academies, all thrilled to be working not only under me, but under the big boss, Chef Timo 'Flaco' Martinez, too. It was a fair kitchen with no undercurrent of danger. No tense silences punctured by angry shouts. Any latent aggression was poured back into the work, it made the food better.

And that year's menu, my last as it would turn out, was one of our best.

As an Argentinean place we were known for our steaks, but we also had a rotating list of excellent specials. Homemade empanadas de camarones, with prawns and bell peppers. Silky pumpkin soup with a toasted provolone roll, baked to be dipped. Breaded veal cutlet topped with melted goats cheese and a bouquet of fresh greens from our roof garden. Crispy pan-fried gnocchi tossed with a tomato malbec reduction. Then Timo's signature dish: *Bife de Flaco,* thin beef steak served with a side of rustic potatoes and a dollop of chimichurri. To finish we had homemade ice cream flavoured with the herbal kick of yerba and honey in a small waffle cup or alfajores, crumbly shortbread cookies over-filled with dulce de leche and dusted with coconut.

The menu was the culmination of 50 years of Chef Timo's career. An Argentinian masterclass delivered by a French woman and an international team, all adopted by London.

Though he was the executive chef, Timo hadn't cooked in years. That was down to me and the team. Our days started at 7am and didn't finish until 11pm. I'd often work through prep, the two hour lunch and then prep again before the four hour dinner service. It was exhausting and thankless and hard, hard work.

But I loved it.

At some point you get acclimated to the busy heat of the kitchen. It becomes a new atmosphere. The only one that you can breathe in. You go to sleep, dream of work, then wake up, the dream and reality overlapping as you rush out of bed to get there on time. You struggle to catch your breath until you have got into your uniform and are standing at your station. Your tired eyes want to settle on the blur of silver, white and black, anything else is too overwhelming. Your ears need the noise of the extractors, the squeak of the doors and the rattle of the pans. And when things are going well, as they had been for several summers, you get the feeling everyone in that kitchen felt the same way as you. Brought together in this intimate kind of busyness. The only place you feel comfortable. At some point you are working so much that the seasoning gets into your skin, so even your sweat has a taste.

And even though we did the work, Timo himself was there most days. Loping around the hallways of the kitchen, walking laps between the smoking area and his office. Always on the phone ignoring the stacks of papers left for him to sign, staring at the faded photos on the walls and listening to rock music that nobody had ever heard of.

But it was at our busiest when his presence had the biggest impact.

'The problem with a groove and a rut is that they both feel the same!' He would shout across the kitchen without breaking stride. His words were like a verbal gear change for the delicate engine of the restaurant. Slapping shoulders of the more junior chefs and walking like Moses through the mass of bodies. He didn't need to taste the food to make it better, he could conduct this orchestra blind. 50 people worked to create the best steaks, pastries and Latin food that London could offer, guided by a distracted wave of his hand. All so he could retain the Michelin star he had spent a career earning.

We all felt the thrill of impressing him when he surprised us with tastings. His rough ringed hand grabbing your shoulder. His tall frame casting a skinny shadow on the plate. The smell of latent cigarettes and coffee on his breath. Somehow never affecting his resilient palate.

He didn't give much feedback. Just a silent thumbs up or a pinched finger and thumb and a nod before he returned to his office, or strode through the double doors into the main room like a cowboy entering a bar at high noon, looking for trouble. To challenge the sycophantic food journalists that worshipped him like a rockstar.

But for me it was different. I'd known Timo since I was a little girl. He would come to my father's farm in Brittany to buy the meat for his legendary Parisian restaurant, Fijo, at the beginning of his celebrity chef career in the early 90s. I would sit fascinated as they talked rapidly in their Argentinian Spanish, losing the trail of the sentences down idiomatic avenues. Now, after a decade of working under him, he had full faith in me to run everything. But even though he would tell me all the time I had reached his level, I never believed him. He had something different. A lifetime of work that left a residue of genius under his fingernails. Impossible to match.

When I requested the morning off for the interview, he didn't ask follow-up questions. He just asked that I was still in for 6am to set-up and check the inventory. He always spoke to me in a mixture of Spanish, French and English, he held each language in his hand like mixed nuts, choosing one to throw into his mouth depending on what suited the phrase the best:

"I can't get up that early anymore, Isita, I'm an old man," he hunched over and did a mock shake of his arms and head, showing fake frailty, I laughed.

"Besides, you haven't taken time off since your mother died *(que descanse en paz).*

"So take the afternoon and evening. I can sort it here."

He winked and I, reluctantly, agreed. I made plans with Ange for after so we could catch up. Talk about the interview, maybe old times.

The team didn't seem to care that I was gone for the day when I told them. They were more excited that he was joining the briefing. Many of them were still starstruck by Timo's presence, seeing him more as a symbol than an actual chef. It was probably good for him to remind them that the old gaucho still had some rope left.

After completing prep I tried to be small and leave through the side as they began their morning meeting. But I lingered to hear if we had anyone important in that day. But Timo noticed me, and shouted:

"¡Mucha merde con la entrevista!", which he punctuated with a vertical slap of his hands.

A few of the Spanish speakers in the kitchen looked up and shot each other knowing, excited looks. There were opportunities for them if I left, both in this kitchen, and perhaps, in my own.

In hindsight, it would have been better if he'd never let me go at all.

* * *

I spotted the car as soon as I left the restaurant. I didn't drive, I lived five minutes from the restaurant and planned on getting the tube, but a tall suited man with salt and pepper hair cocked his head at me as I entered the street.

Is this for me, I asked?

"Yes, Ms Maldona."

I was shocked when he said my name.

"I'm George, from Primagen Industries, I'm here to take you to your interview," he said, tapping a badge on his pocket, a swooping P and I interlocked on the Primagen logo. His name and photo underneath.

Wow. I said it involuntarily, shrugging with surprise as he opened the door for me.

I had detected a hint of an Iberian accent in George, though he'd said his name the English way, so asked him when we were sat in the car:

¿Eres español?

"Spanish? No, no, I am here, from England," he replied with a smile. I didn't know whether to talk to the side of his head or match his eyes in the mirror.

Oh, of course. I let us drift back into silence as we drove across the city, taking roads that tourists didn't use. The capillaries of brick and glass that keep the body of London going. The place that even after a decade of service I still didn't feel at home in.

After fifteen minutes we pulled up to a square.

"It's that building." He pointed with a smile.

Thank you. How much do I owe? I asked, swinging my bag round onto my lap.

"Oh no, it's all covered Ms Maldona."

I thanked him again, and stepped out. George watched me until I found the door for Primagen, smiling and waving from the car when I turned to check he was still there.

The door's glass was frosted, but it buzzed open as I approached. White marble floors and an empty bamboo desk that jutted out from a matching wall. There was a large floor plan, with space for 20 levels, but only Primagen's logos on each of the entries, listing their different departments. On floor 12 I saw what I was looking for:

11 PRIMAGEN INDUSTRIES - *BIOMES & MAINTENANCE*

12 PRIMAGEN INDUSTRIES - *GROWTH & MARKETING DIVISION*

13 PRIMAGEN INDUSTRIES - *BIOENGINEERING LABORATORY ALPHA*

A lift at the end of the room opened and a man, he could have been George's son, walked towards me. He confirmed my name, gave me a badge and wrote some notes on his clipboard as he eyed me up and down. Then he walked me through the barriers and guided me into the lift.

"Floor 12. Straight ahead. Conference room 1, Ms Maldona". He pressed some buttons on his tablet and the doors shut with a whirr.

The lift was all mirrors and no buttons, but it began to move on its own. I looked at the four angles of myself, going on forever. I pushed down the baby hairs at the corner of my hairline and twisted the curls at the back. I felt uncomfortable out of my uniform and poked at the sides of my jeans. I traced the contours of my right side, a pocket on my glute with no muscle at all, dystrophied to a dent. A fall that left me lopsided. The kind of thing you forget about until you're staring at yourself in a full-length mirror in trousers much tighter than when you first bought them. My hip was like a collapsed meringue, and the cracks showed across the rest of my body too. My skin was dry, I was pale, and had bags that I tried to rub away, a last minute attempt at fixing my tiredness. All the consequences of the summer season and ten years of no sleep.

The lift opened to a hallway with a door to a boardroom. The corridors forked around it left and right. I focused and walked towards it. Every interview was an opportunity, I reminded myself. Took a deep breath. Knocked twice.

ELIZABETH CHAMPION

The Hardest Word

Synopsis

A sixth former breaks her silence and accuses a classmate of raping her, compelling her mother and grandmother to confront silences of their own.

London, 2020: Emily sleeps with Fraser at a party. She asks him to stop, but he doesn't. The next day, she demands an apology. Fraser is scared and refuses. Emily goes to the police.

Mexico, 1994: Nicola, Emily's mother, has sex with a guy she meets while travelling. She asks him to stop, but he doesn't. Nicola decides to pretend it never happened.

London, 1967: Dorothy, Nicola's mother, invites Colin to her bedsit after a date. At the last minute, she says she doesn't want sex, but he carries on. Dorothy terms it a passionate seduction. Dorothy marries Colin.

When Nicola and Dorothy learn what happened to Emily, they are secretly perturbed by the similarities between her experience and theirs. Dorothy, now a widow, refuses to accept that Colin raped her. At a family dinner, she implies that Emily was not really raped either. Emily says she no longer wants to see Dorothy.

The police drop Emily's case. Emily says she wants to move on, but Nicola knows that rape cannot be forgotten. She fears that someone as forthright as Emily won't be happy staying silent. She encourages Emily to start campaigning against sexual violence, and after some resistance, Emily agrees. Her friends, who previously sided with Fraser, now side with her.

Nicola is inspired to open up about her own rape. Dorothy, still wanting to defend Colin, reacts unsympathetically. Furious with herself for upsetting Nicola, Dorothy finally forces herself to acknowledge that Colin raped her. She phones Nicola and Emily and makes peace.

Fraser, meanwhile, sinks into denial. Friendless and bitter, he alternates between hatred and longing for Emily. All he wants is to forget.

Elizabeth Champion

THE HARDEST WORD

June 2020

1

It is hot today; a heavy, sweaty inescapable sort of heat that drags at Fraser as he climbs to Mum's study. He would do anything for a breeze on his face, cold water on his skin, a glass of iced squash – he could go and get one, but then he'd be late.

Outside the door, he pauses, wiping his forehead on his t-shirt. Mum is on the phone; she's using her work voice, sharper and more commanding than her home voice.

"Basically you're telling me the Home Office have fucked up, and they want me to make it seem like they haven't fucked up?"

Fraser pushes the door; Mum swivels round, couched in her brand-new ergonomic office chair, phone pressed to her ear. Her top half is dressed for court – weighty black gown, thick horsehair wig, stiff winged collar: her lower half is ready for the beach – red linen shorts, purple flip-flops, neat square toenails painted glossy pink. Fraser gestures at what she's wearing and looks at her like 'what on earth?' She grins, beckoning him into the room with a jerk of her head. Fraser creeps across the carpet towards the daybed in the corner.

"If the Home Sec has been consulted then I don't have much choice, do I?"

He sits, taking his phone from his pocket and placing it beside him. The bedcover is furry; it sticks to the sweat behind his knees.

Mum stretches back, itching her scalp where her wig meets her forehead. "Ok but tell them to have an answer ready. I don't want to piss Cecil off any more than necessary."

Fraser flaps the front of his t-shirt to try and get some air inside. He looks around the room – basic white Ikea bookshelves housing Mum's law books; white walls with no pictures; black bin liners slouched against the daybed, full of clothes he's grown out of. He hardly ever comes up here, mainly because he doesn't need to, but also because this room unsettles him. It's part study, part spare room, part dumping ground – a room with an identity crisis, trying to do too many things at once and doing none of them well.

The window is open, but the air it's admitting isn't cooling. Heat radiates in wavy lines off the red-tiled rooves of the houses behind. TV aerials glint in the sun. Someone is using some kind of noisy machine in a garden nearby. It sputters and growls like a beast on a leash.

Mum cackles mischievously into the phone. She crosses her legs, bare in her shorts. Fraser is glad that Jonno can't see her like this. Jonno would say her outfit was kinky; he'd make some shit joke about dressing up as a judge and 'hammering her with his gavel.'

Mum looks down at her watch. "Oops, it's almost ten, we'd better log on … Yup, ok. Brilliant, bye." Mum thrusts her phone down on her desk, picks up her water bottle and glugs some back.

"What's happening?"

"Total cock up," says Mum. She slams the water bottle down and clicks at her laptop. She has arranged it on top of *Bennion on Statutory Interpretation* and a couple of other chunky law books so the screen is level with her face. "That was the woman from TSol. There'll probably be an adjournment."

"What?" says Fraser. "Why?"

"I'll explain later. Sorry, I know it's a pain. This would have been an interesting hearing for you to watch."

Mum has switched to her home voice, more girlish than her work voice. Her vowels have become flatter, and Fraser can detect a faint nasality, a weak echo of how his po-po and gung-gung used to speak.

Dad likes to tease Mum about her various voices, but she says it's normal to alter the way you speak for different audiences. She says Dad is the freak, not her. 'You sound permanently like you're auditioning to join the royal family,' she tells him. Dad just laughs. 'I sound posh because I am posh,' he always replies, 'Why should I hide who I am?'

The person with the noisy machine outside is really going for it now. It's whining and buzzing like a swarm of angry hornets.

"Bloody hell!" Mum slams the window shut with a dull thud. "Every time I have a hearing, some moron decides to trim his hedges or power-wash his patio or something. Every sodding time!"

She looks back at her screen. The light is shining on it, but Fraser can just make out the waiting symbol going round and round. She takes off her heavy, black-framed glasses and rubs the bridge of her nose. Without them, her face seems exposed somehow, delicate. Fraser thinks of Jonno again, all those stupid fucking comments he makes about looking up her picture on her chambers' website and jerking off. Fraser rubs the scar on his lip where they operated when he was a baby.

Mum puts her glasses back on – serious, heavyweight glasses for a serious, heavyweight lawyer. Fraser feels a sudden surge of pride. Who else amongst his friends can say that their mum is a QC, a human rights specialist who acts for the Government on some of their most high-profile cases? She started at the bottom, the child of immigrants. They grafted, she grafted, she got into Oxford, and now, according to Dad, she is tipped to become the next Treasury Counsel, the Government's top civil barrister. As far as Fraser can tell, Jonno's mum does nothing except buy stuff and get her nails done. Sam says his mum does freelance marketing or something, but Fraser has never seen any evidence – she always seems to be baking when he goes to Sam's house, that or taking their dog out.

"We're starting. You stay out of sight, ok?" Mum sits up straight, adjusts her wig, then switches on her camera.

Fraser leans forwards to get a better look at the faces appearing on the screen, but he can't really see.

A voice comes out of the laptop. "You're on mute, my lord." The woman speaking sounds weary, like this has happened to her a million times before. She has a raspy Essex accent that seems to catch in her throat as she talks. The court usher, perhaps?

"Is that any better?" booms the judge. His voice is rich, resonant, unashamedly upper-class – a lot like Dad's voice, in fact.

"We can hear you clearly now, my lord," says Mum. She is using her court voice, which is like her work voice, but smoother and silkier. Her vowels are as round as oranges; all hint of nasality has gone. "Before we get started, my lord, I should make you aware that my son is with me, observing the hearing for a school work-experience project. I trust there are no objections?"

"None from me," says the judge. "If we were in a courtroom any Tom, Dick or Harry could wander in and watch. What do you say, Mr Wade?"

"No objection, my lord." Mr Wade must be the barrister representing the terrorist whose case is being heard. His voice is whiny and monotone. Fraser wonders if he and the judge are wearing shorts under their robes like Mum.

"Good. Right, to business," says the judge. "The hearing can't possibly go ahead following this morning's communications, can it, Ms Liu?"

Mum leans on her elbow towards the screen. "It is the Secretary of State's position that the hearing should proceed as planned, my lord."

The judge pelts out a laugh. "Is it, by George?"

"As you are aware, my lord, Covid has created unprecedented challenges for my client." Mum continues on, retaining her upright posture, speaking in a lulling, musical way that Fraser imagines could convince anyone to believe anything. She says the word 'exculpatory' a lot. It's a term Fraser has heard Mum and Dad use – he's certain they've explained it to him, but right now, in all this heat, he cannot remember what 'exculpatory' means. He stifles a yawn and glances down at his phone.

A WhatsApp from Emily Shastri. What? He stares at the name. Why the fuck is Emily Shastri messaging him? She has never messaged him before. She has never even spoken to him except to say 'hi' or 'bye.' He taps on the message.

<Hey, hope you're surviving lockdown and not dying of boredom. Just wondering if you've seen the class lists for next year? I had no idea that we're doing the exact same A-levels! Isn't that wild?!!>

He blinks. He blinks again. This message cannot actually be real. He must be having some psychotic daydream induced by spending too much time at home, playing too much *Resident Evil,* and watching too much porn, way too much porn. Didn't they used to say that wanking could drive you mad? It has happened; it has finally happened. He has lost touch with reality. He's rubbing his scar.

The message must be a hoax. Jonno and Sam have probably set up a fake account in her name. He peers at the message; it seems genuine. There's a picture of her next to her name – a headshot. He taps on it to make it larger. Fuck, she's fit. He feels it like a slap round the face, like hands around his neck. She is, basically, perfect – so perfect that he finds it hard to believe that she is a person he knows, who came to his party last year. She is kind of too perfect to describe. He could label her component parts – her lustrous dark hair, her golden skin, her huge, long-lashed eyes – but that wouldn't come close to capturing her. It would make her sound beautiful in a predictable way, turn her into something obvious, when she's not obvious at all.

There must have been an email from school. The email will tell him if it's true, if he really is doing the same A-levels as her. He searches for his inbox, his thumb sticky against the screen. The whiny barrister is talking now, saying something about Pakistan.

There it is: an email entitled 'King George's School Sixth Form Induction Information.' It has various attachments: 'Timetable for online induction day 2020'; 'Sixth form dress code'; 'Subject lists.' He opens this last attachment and scans it. P for Pearce, Fraser. S for Shastri, Emily. His name. Her name. Together. English. Maths. Latin. Greek.

He wants to jump up and shout. It physically hurts to stay still. Not only are they doing the same subjects; they are in the same sets. Each subject, four double periods per week. Each double period an hour and a half. Six hours of classes per subject per week. Twenty-four hours a week with Emily Shastri. He'd heard that she was joining his school for sixth form; he'd hoped that that they might have a few classes together – but this?

"I'm in agreement with Mr Wade," says the judge, "An adjournment is the only possible course."

Obviously, Fraser is being stupid. It makes no difference whether he has one class a week with Emily, or five, or a hundred. She's not suddenly going to start fancying him just because they are studying the same subjects. All that's going to happen is that he's going to spend the next two years gawping at her. He will learn nothing; he will fail his A-levels; he will not get into Oxford; he will not follow his parents to the Bar. His life is ruined. He might as well give up now.

"May I message to my client to clarify instructions, my lord?" says Mum.

"I think that's a jolly sensible idea, Ms Liu."

Mum is tapping furiously at her phone. Is Emily looking at her phone as well? She has probably noticed that Fraser has opened her message. If he doesn't respond quickly, it will seem like he's not pleased about her news.

He starts typing. <Hey, how ru doing? Just saw the lists. That's amazing that we have so many classes together! …> He sounds too enthusiastic, like he fancies her. Delete, delete, delete.

He tries again. <Hey, how r u doing? I'm surviving lockdown ok, hope u r too. Just looked at the lists. That's so crazy!! I had no idea either. What are the chances?> He reads over what he's written. It's better, more neutral. He presses send and is immediately beset by fear. The message was boring, too generic and vanilla; he should have said something to make her laugh. He must send a follow up. What would Sam say to a girl in this situation? Fraser pulls himself up tall, trying to imagine himself with Sam's confidence and golden curls and effortless charm.

<Great taste in A-levels btw> he types. A bit cringe, maybe? Fraser can't think of anything else. He breathes in and presses send.

Mum stops typing and glowers at her phone, tapping her fingernails on the desk.

Two blue ticks on the side of Fraser's messages. Emily has opened them, but she's not typing. Mum taps her nails faster. The hedge trimmer whirrs outside.

Emily must have thought his messages were weird – too presumptive coming from someone like him, too familiar. She has decided to ignore them.

It seems to have got even hotter. He feels like he's made of wax, melting in the heat; sweat and hope seeps out of him. A bee bashes into the windowpane, then again, and again, and again.

Mum smiles down at her phone, then sits up straight. "I have received an answer from my client, my lord."

Lucky Mum. She got an answer. She's saying something to the judge about social distancing, something about the Ministry of Justice. Fraser keeps his eyes on his phone. Emily's typing. Yes, she's typing!

Her reply flashes up. <Lol. We both have great taste in A levels!>

She wrote 'lol'! He made her laugh! He made Emily Shastri laugh! There's a tingly, bursting feeling inside his chest. She's still typing.

<I guess I'll 'see' u at the induction on Monday. Shame we can't do it irl>

Is she saying she wishes she could see *him* in real life? Of course not – she's just being polite.

<I know! I'm so sick of doing stuff online> Send. Check him out, chatting away with Emily Shastri, all chilled, all casual, like he messages phenomenally fit girls all the time.

(Chapter continues)

HIGHLY COMMENDED

CHARLOTTE COLE

Babygirl

Synopsis

It's 2013, May is twenty-nine, barely adult, unemployed again, and stuck in the flat her family has always lived in. Exhausted from the neglect they've suffered, May's Nana, Mum and beloved older sister Agnes have let go, disappearing into the walls, doors, and beds. They have left May behind, almost alone.

In a grey, suburban wasteland on the outskirts of a southern town, May is the sole guardian of her only remaining relative, her teenage niece, Babygirl. They raise each other in a liminal existence, evading interrogation from school, and the overhanging cloud of social services.

Babygirl grows up quickly; her adolescence is unforgiving on them both. May soon understands she is failing as a carer, but, just as she thinks of letting go, she begins to see the shadows of her Mum, Nana and Agnes around the flat. Their ghosts are on an infinite loop, forced to repeat the moment they abandoned May. Together again, their presence swells as May seeks comfort from their whispers. Unable to cope with reality, May retreats into her own childhood.

She is taken to her earliest memories, retracing her steps from year to year. She watches her family navigate an uncertain life where men are transient, women are survivors and Agnes is everything. As she reaches the moments closest to Agnes' desertion, May notices similar signs in Babygirl's behaviour, and fights to keep her grounded.

Across two timelines, May searches for meaning in the generational curse she's inherited, and seeks to break the cycle. In the end, it's Babygirl who teaches May to let go, releasing the ghosts trapped in the house, and joining them in final freedom. This is not a ghost story, but a story about learning to live with your ghosts.

August 1995

Nana May has a way with corned beef. She fries it slow and low, so the flecks of milky jelly melt away, crisping up the meat in the pan. We use salad cream or brown sauce with it, never ketchup, which Nana tells us is tacky American nonsense. She's making four corned beef sandwiches, then another four egg and cress with a bit of mustard. She is using the good bread, from the bakery, not even pre-sliced, and as we're doing a trip in a car, she leaves the crusts on.

'Crusts keep the shape of a sandwich, Little May. Never travel with a crustless egg mayo, you're asking for trouble,' she says as she lays out slices across the whole kitchen counter, lined in clingfilm.

Mum's taking out her hot rollers at the kitchen table, her bare feet up on a chair, airing her newly painted hot pink toenails. I'm stood opposite, holding a metal bowl filled with chopped up egg waiting to be mixed with mayonnaise. I'm already wearing my swimsuit under my shorts and t-shirt so I don't have to be naked on the beach later, but the faint smell of old chlorine is mixing with egg and making me carsick before we're even off. I try not to breathe too much, patiently waiting for direction from Nana.

'Ok four spoons of mayo in that love. Be careful not to mush it when you stir it. We want sandwich filler not baby food. Good. Now pop it on four of these slices. I'll do the cress.'

Mum raises her eyebrows.

'Eight sandwiches? We're only going away for one night, and we're going to the chippy for dinner.'

'You never know, Juney. Anything can happen with that drive, anything, and on a bank holiday? Stop it. We could break down on the A31, with two little ones in the car no less, then you'll be grateful for it,' she looks at the pile of white bread sandwiches with real worry. 'I'll make a couple cheese and pickle too. To be safe.'

'Christ Mum, why not do half a dozen Spam while you're at it.'

Nana May puts down her butter knife, turns to Mum and says, 'I would never do a Spam sandwich Juney, and you know it,' she turns to me as I spoon mounds of goo onto the buttered squares. 'There's an inelegance to Spam, May.'

I once ate cold Spam out of the tin and threw it up in the bath later, so I nod in agreement. I put the bowl in the sink and rinse it; milky water laced with egg floaters spirals down the drain. We're moving onto the cheese and pickle, so I get what we need from the fridge for Nana to start preparing. She gets on with it alone, so I pack up the rest of the bits in the cool bag and regular bag. I tesselate juice cartons in the bottom of the cool bag, laying them on top of blue ribbed ice packs. They'll make the cold base for the sandwiches. I stuff the regular bag with my favourite part of family trips: pickled onion Space Raiders, mint and orange Puffin bars from ASDAs, and a red net of satsumas. Mum is watching me, beaming.

'Aren't you an angel.'

Nana tugs on my earlobe, 'She's a blessing. And so is that other one, in her own way.'

'If she'd take two seconds away from that mirror, she'd hear it for herself.'

Agnes had promised to help me with the sandwiches, but she felt fat in her bikini and went to rearrange her outfit for the day. She's fifteen with big boobs, which she says belong in a serious bikini. Mine are flat and belong in a shiny swimsuit with frills on the leg holes. Now That's What I Call Music 95 is coming through our bedroom door, so I know not to go in and get her. She'll come out when she's ready. Her music is mixing with the Robson & Jerome tape Nana hasn't stopped playing in the kitchen for a two weeks. Mum spots the clock.

'Jesus fucking Christ it's already eight. We'll never get there in time to get a good spot. Where is she. Ag? Agnes? Get your bottom in here now, we need to go.'

Ag appears in a new red bikini, covered with Mum's sheer linen shirt, unbuttoned and open, and ripped cut off shorts, also unbuttoned with the top rolled down. Her shoes look like they're made of cloth and nice rope. Nana gives her a once over with a raised eyebrow.

'You made your bed madam?'

'Yeah.'

'Hospital corners?'

'Yes ma'am,' she salutes.

'Help your sister with the bags, let's be on our way.'

In Bournemouth, we find a spot in what feels like the middle of the beach. The sun here is hotter than the sun in Eastleigh, it feels brighter on the eyes. Ag puts up the umbrella and the windbreaker, Mum digs a hole for the cooler, pops it in and gets out a beer. I laugh, and Nana throws us both a dirty look.

'Oh please,' Mum says, turning to Nana, 'you think I'm going to be at the beach sober? You're fucking mad.'

'You have a filthy mouth June. Get me an egg and cress while you're in there.'

We settle fast, Mum and Nana on the fold-out chairs, me and Ag on a carpet of bath towels. Seagulls harass people with ice cream, children dig holes, all clouds burn away and leave us with an entirely blue sky. Mum glistens with a layer of factor 50, hiding under an umbrella *to save her complexion.* Nana is splayed out in her chair, four mottled brown limbs spilling out of a mint green swimsuit. Her belly and boobs are pastel mountains, rising and falling from her sagging cloth seat as she breathes in and out.

'Ooh it's nice to get sea air in the lungs isn't it,' Nana says, sucking on a green Superking.

We all say, 'yeah. Lovely.'

'It does smell a bit like piss though,' says Ag.

'Don't be crass,' Mum replies.

'She's right, it honks. It's the seaweed.' says Nana.

'It's seaweed and ozone,' I tell her.

'I thought that was what's giving us skin cancer,' says Mum.

'That's the ozone layer.'

'Right. And why is it giving us cancer?' she replies.

'It's not.'

'It is, I saw it on the telly.'

'It's true love, it was on the BBC,' Nana says with a nod.

'No. The ozone layer protects us from the sun, which can give us skin cancer. The ozone layer is disappearing because we use too much hairspray, so we're getting skin cancer more. Mrs Sheffield told us.'

'Oh. Right,' Mum says, pulling out her packet of B&Hs and a Snoopy lighter. 'Well it can't have gone far.'

'How do you mean?' I say.

'Well it smells properly of piss here, so it can't be all be gone can it.'

We spend the day on rotation. Two near the bags, two down in the sea. Ag and I went first, then Mum and Nana. Soon Mum gets bored and just wants to read her magazines. Ag covers herself head to toe in tanning oil and lies down, splayed out like star fish on the towels. I desperately don't want Ag to sleep. I want to swim with her; I even brought my arm bands with the shark fins on so we could go out deeper. I eat a melting orange Puffin, lying on my side, staring at Ag in an effort to telepathically wake her. Nana is behind me on her chair, fanning herself with a Reader's Digest.

'Pop your jelly shoes on love. Let's leave these two to melt.'

Nana and I sit at the edge of the sea, waves falling over our feet. The tide comes in stronger and goes all the way up our legs. The sea is blue, clear and soft, like her voice as she tells me stories.

'Me and my big sister would come here all the time. We skipped school and hitchhiked every summer.'

'On your own?'

'Yes. Nancy was brave.'

'You lived with her.'

'Oh yes, until I got married to your grandad. And then again, after.'

'I didn't know grandad.'

'No, love. No you didn't. And I thank God for it.'

'Do you miss him?'

She doesn't answer, but looks out over the sea. A group of kids are playing around a buoy. Their laughter sounds miles away.

'Did I ever meet Nancy?'

'She saw you the day you were born, but went soon after. It was all quite sudden,' she moves her hand closer to mine and loops our little fingers together. Her voice is quiet and grey. 'She was always the brave one. Not me. But then I got to move in with you didn't I love. God I was glad to get out of that place.'

'Why did you want to leave it?'

'What?'

'Why did you leave your house? Our place is so small.'

'Well I wanted to give you girls a good upbringing, be close to you. Anyway, I couldn't stay there.'

'Didn't you like it?'

'Yes I liked it. But it felt crowded.'

'But you lived alone?'

'Yes.'

'So how was it crowded?'

She looks down, away from me.

'Listen to me rattling on. It's all in the past May love. Dead and buried.'

I don't understand, but Nana is pursing her lips. She's wearing sunglasses but I think she's holding back tears. I pat her hand.

'We get to look after each other now, don't we.'

'Yes love. We're cut from the same cloth, you and I. We have to keep this family together. Fortitude, May. Fortitude.'

I don't know what this means, but probably that I need to be more patient with Ag. I shuffle over right up close to Nana, and lean into her warm skin. It smells like sun cream, salt, and old oily perfume. Up close her skin is a light brown field, with white and dark blotches woven together like lace. I thread my arm through hers, rest my head on her shoulder, and watch a young boy jumping through the breakwater. He's pale, freckled and unafraid. All on his own, he dives into the collapsing waves, swims out and swims back in to do it all over again. Ag calls for us to come back. It's time for tea.

The pier is busy; we are a swarm of colour-pop flies hovering over a hot bin. I hold onto Ag's hand as she drags me between sunburnt beach goers. The air is fried doughnuts and candyfloss, and the pink-green-yellow lights from the toy sellers blur as we run past them. We run faster and faster, Ag expertly jumping in all the right gaps in the crowd. I run so fast I'm barely touching the ground. With Ag's sure and nimble feet leading the way, we weave through the busiest part, between the henna and hair braiding stalls. I trust her, so close my eyes and follow the feel of her pull. Ag swerves, I open my eyes and we're running straight for a big blue sign. *Fishcotheque*.

The floor's a muddy shade of beige, a bit sticky under my jelly shoes. Against the yellowing floor, their blueish glitter looks sea-green. The chippy smells of fish, oil and bleach. I sit on a plastic chair at the back while Mum orders. I feel sand in my bum crack, it's itchy and will be sore later, but know it's not polite to sort it out inside, even if we are kind of still at the beach.

Nana May gets a mini cod and nothing else because she doesn't have much of an appetite these days, Mum has her chips with a Styrofoam pot of mustard-yellow curry sauce. Ag and I pool our scampi, tear up a battered sausage into chunks, mix them all with our portion of chips, douse it in vinegar and salt, and shake it in the box. We fill the empty spaces with blobs of tartar sauce, burger sauce, and ketchup. I have both of the pickled gherkins because Ag doesn't like them, but we take turns swapping the candy-striped cans of cream soda and shandy. The four of us sit in silence, lined up on the rough sea wall, legs swinging a few inches above the sand. The seagulls are distracted by the doughnut man taking out his binbags and the day begins to leave us. The air cools. People pack away their umbrellas and towels, pink sun, pink sky, pink skin. Ag lets me take the last chips, the wettest ones, perfectly soaked in sauce.

Full and laughing, I sit on Ag's lap and we take guesses at people's lives as they pass by. One man, ginger, tall, on his own eating chips, is definitely a pedo. The man on the beach scanning for metal with a thing that looks like a thin hoover is probably already rich. The group of boys playing football down by the tideline are all ugly and therefore virgins, according to Ag. I ask her how she knows.

'You can literally just tell, it's like a birthmark.'

I am terrified this is true, and remind myself to check for birthmarks when I'm having a bath. Through all this, Ag and I are actively ignoring what's next to us. Mum and Nana are quietly fighting, trying to stop us from seeing their pointing fingers by turning their backs to us. There's a lot of shrugging, sighing and shaking of heads, in a way that can only be done by mums. Nana says *fine fine fine* to Mum in a low voice through gritted teeth, but then speaks openly, with a happy lilt in her tone to me and Ag.

'Right then. Say nuh'night to your Mum girls.'

I stare. Ag laughs and shakes her head. Nana eats leftover chips with her eyebrows raised. Mum swings her legs over the wall, straightening her sundress with a wiggle of her hips. She roots around in her straw bag, buried up to the elbow, feeling for something, eyes closed. Her arm reemerges, her hand like a claw machine clasped around a fluorescent pink heart shaped compact mirror. With her face in its reflection, she reapplies a coral lip. She doesn't need the mirror for bronzer, she just applies it on the high points of her face. She smiles at me with a *what do you think then* face and I give her a thumbs up. Ag is staring her down.

'So you're off then?' she says.

'I'm meeting someone, yes,' Mum replies.

'And when did you plan this?'

'Absolutely none of your business to be honest Agnes love.'

'Is it a man?'

'Less of that.'

'So it's a man. You're leaving your kids on the beach for a man.'

'She's not leaving us,' I say, punching Ag in the arm. 'She's just going out for a bit.'

Ag gives me a look between anger and *what do you even mean*; it's frighteningly similar to Mum's.

JENNIFER COLES

Flotsam

Synopsis

Amber lives with her five-year-old daughter, Lexi, in a studio flat in Margate. Having grown up in care, she has no support from her family. The father of her child is trapped in a hazy world of heroin. Compared with him, Amber is doing well. Her wayward days at art school are over and her only vice now is Valium, which she buys online. However, she exists in a bubble and by most people's standards, she's sinking. Denial and isolation keep her stuck in a messy, unreal world of pillows, cuddles, bubble baths and sleep.

When she wakes up to a knock on the door, reality intrudes. A policeman informs her that Lexi was found wandering the streets alone at night. Social services are called in and an assessment begins. Amber works as hard as she can to clean up her act. Lexi enrols in a primary school and Amber joins a detox group. Both are expanding their worlds and making new relationships, but these new relationships take Amber out of her comfort zone and she begins to feel she is out of her depth. Under pressure, she finds herself telling different versions of her life story to different people, getting tangled in a web of lies. All she wants is to give her daughter a better life, but her self-doubt makes her sabotage this intention, sending her spiralling down.

1.

Wake up mummy it's mornin.

Eyes open. Bright white light. Eyes shut tight.

Please don't point that torch at me.

Red explosions on closed lids, silent bombs. She's scorched the retinas.

You torture me, you know.

I hear a giggle in the dark.

Mummy look, look, look.

Eyes open, cautious slits. The torch is under Lexi's chin, lighting up her gummy grin, two new gaps in her milk teeth. I sigh, rub my sandy eyes, then close the lids again and drop my head, a dead weight on my neck.

But it's morneen.

Her pronunciation bothers me.

It's ning. Morning. Say it?
Ning.
That's right.

My mouth is dry. I reach for bedside water, something bitter in it, soap? Lexi, what have you done?

As if she's done nothing at all, she leaps across the floor with the grace of a lamb, torch in hand, illuminating soup bowls, books and Jenga blocks, Lego bricks and oil paints strewn like flotsam on a sea of unwashed clothes. She manages not to topple the jam jar of cigarette ash with her toe as she approaches, crouches next to the bed and plants a kiss and a kiss on my head.

So, she loves me a little today.

She leans in close and buzzes in my ear.

Mmmooorninnng.

Oh, the tingling, deep in the drum. Unreachable tickle she's given me there. My gnarled fingernail is working away at the wax.

Give me that torch.

The torch was a birthday gift from her dad. He chose it to punish me, I'm sure. Lexi clutches the thing to her chest.

I said give it to me.

The light comes wheeling through the darkness and whacks me on the arm.

Ouch.
Oops.
You could have hit my head.

I shine the light on the clock on the wall. It's not even quarter to five.

For god's sake, let me rest.
Boreen.
It's ring. Boring.
Borin.
Never mind, you're tired.
I am not that.
You must be. You stayed up half the night.

We can't go on like this. She wakes me up at intervals. The dark hours are divided into snatches of interrupted sleep. I can hardly remember going to bed, it seems so long ago. There was a bedtime story, I think, about a hungry caterpillar or tiger who came to tea, then we had the usual drama of pyjamas where I chase Lexi around the bed with clothes she refuses to put on and now, again, she wakes me up before the dawn. I'm depleted, merely the husk of myself.

Shush, a rustling. Lexi freezes whilst I scan the floor with the torch until I spot it: there, in the clutter, a Tesco bag moving alive. Lexi pounces and the daily dance begins, a kerfuffle of Walker's crisps and crepe paper in talcum powder clouds.

The mess invades me. A nauseous wave moves through me at the thought of sorting it out. I cleaned the flat yesterday, I'm sure, or was it the day before? Every time I try, some insidious force seems to hatch a plan to sabotage my work.

I open the quilt, wide as a wing.

Come on, snuggle in. You need your sleep too.
Do not need you.

Rejection punches me in the stomach. She doesn't love me so much after all.

I swaddle myself in the quilt and roll over, but what's this? A damp patch. I give it a sniff, throw off the cover and switch on the lamp.

What happened here?

Lexi is playing with her doll or pretending to play.

I'm not angry with you.

Her cheeks turn pink beneath her freckles as she mumbles.

I did dream.
I can't hear you.
I did dream of the sliver-green sea.
It's silver-green.

I correct her, then regret it. I can see she's already ashamed. This isn't the first time she's had an accident of this kind, but it is the first time I tell her it used to happen to me at her age.

You?
So I know you'll grow out of it too.

What I don't tell her is that I didn't grow out of it for years. I never went to sleepovers in case I might wake up in sheets of shame.

Pain shoots up my spine as I strip the bed. I'm heavy as rock and yet too slight, my ribs and shoulder blades protruding. I seem to have become some incongruity of bone and stone. What was that sculpture I saw at the British Museum when I was free and childless, when I moved about the city, breathing it in? That statue stolen from the Parthenon, shipped over, weathered, chipped, that decapitated sea nymph dancing wildly in the wind…

I peel off Lexi's wet pyjamas, wondering why I didn't smell the piss until my nose was pressed against the sheet. Am I numb with fatigue? Now that I've caught a whiff, I can't smell anything else.

The bathroom light is bright. My sallow face rejects me in the mirror. My copper hair has lost its sheen and gives the impression of rust. I share the bath with so many yellow rubber ducks and Lexi, who squeezes a sponge on her head and laughs as the bubbles trickle down, but I can't laugh with her, not now. I can't even bring myself to smile.

I had the foresight, at least, to buy more bedding on the credit card. For once, Lexi doesn't reject the pyjamas I choose for her. It's half-past five. There's still time to catch a stretch of sleep before the daylight intrudes.

I hear a clatter in the kitchen.

Icky here.

Lexi has plunged a hand in the sink.

Don't do that. Knives in there.

I grab her arm and pull it out. She looks at me, affronted, as though I've injured her. I only want to keep her safe. She holds her stomach.

I'm hungry.
It's too early.
Rumble grumbling there.

This she knows will work. I'd never deny her food.

All right, a mug of milk, then bed.
No, porridge, not too hot.
Says Goldilocks.

The audacity. I never would have dared to make demands of my mother like that. I want to give Lexi the freedom I didn't have myself, but she's so brazen. Maybe I'm too soft.

I turn away to stir the oats on the stove and Lexi scribbles all over her face with a pen. We've just had a bath. It's an endless cycle. Clean up, then make a mess. I feel like Sisyphus pushing a rock up a hill, then watching it roll down again, on repeat. I take a breath. I need a smoke.

I dish out the porridge and make a rollie. Lexi holds up a spoonful for me.

I'm not hungry, darling.

Her face droops and her offering plops in the bowl. I spark a light and inhale. The nicotine sends a rush to my head and down through my veins, but Lexi coughs and the pleasure is gone. I don't care what I do to my own lungs, but Lexi's must be spared.

The window out to the back is stuck. There's a knack to it. I have to pull the handle hard, then push. The cold air nips my nose, but the rest of me is warm inside the sheepskin coat my mother left. It was far too big for me then, now it's too tight.

Frost glistens on the fire escape, cast iron steps leading down to the garden which belongs to the couple downstairs. In the daytime, I might see Mr Wittering bustling with a tea tray or Mrs Wittering hacking at the weeds, but there's no one out there now, except for a fox, disturbing a hedge, slinking across the grass as if he's guilty, or quietly pleased with himself.

The sky throws out a handful of gulls, beating the air with their wings. Why are they up so early in the morning? How do they find their way in the pitch? Why do they always sound so sad?

White wisps of breath whirl into the black sky like a ghost, the ghost of Barbara Hepworth, perhaps. I think of her when I smoke. She left a cigarette smouldering on her bedside table as she drifted off to sleep for the last time and I wonder, was there a moment when she woke up in the heat? Could she have tried to walk through the fire on her arthritic hip or might she have stayed there, paralysed with fear, praying that the smoke would choke her before the flames could roast her flesh? It doesn't bear thinking about and yet, I think of it often, I think of it now. At least it helps me to remember to put my embers out. I squash my rollie on the step. It sizzles in the frost.

I climb inside and wrestle with the window, but it won't close all the way. A wheezing wind comes through the gap. Maybe the hinges are starting to rust. A job for the landlord, I suppose, when I've tidied up. For now, I'll stuff the gap with a scarf to diminish the draft.

Lexi is waving her spoon in the air, swinging her legs off the chair.

We go to the beach today?
We can go to the beach.
Now?
Wait for the light, at least.

She speaks in a word-stream, dreaming of kites in the clouds and castles in the sand covered in shells and where does it end? I was so keen to teach her to speak when all she could do was cry and cry, but now she has so many thoughts, so uncontained.

I can see from the dips and mounds in her bowl that she's hardly eaten a thing.

Don't play with your food. You know it upsets me.

She acts as though I'm not in the room. I tap her bowl. She gives me a flick of the wrist and puts on a voice.

I'm not hungry, darling.

She's mocking me. Heat surges through my nerves.

You said you were rumbling, said you were grumbling. You kept me out of bed.

She sweeps her porridge onto the floor. It looks like puke on my poetry books. Her chair squeaks as she scurries off. She's faster than me, but in this flat, there's nowhere to hide. I chase her until she trips and falls. There's a pause, then a sob, but it lacks conviction. I know her cries, I've studied them for years.

Bed. Now.

Lexi does as she's told. It must be the tone of my voice. I switch off the lamp and watch the red shapes fade on my closed eyes.

Lexi is stiff lying beside me until I hold her, then she softens in my arms. She smells like apricots and cream. When she snoozes, she sounds just like the sea breathing in, breathing out.

It doesn't last. Soon her elbows are jabbing my ribs. I give up. I've tried everything. I'm at the end of my rope.

Do what you want then. I can't force you to sleep.
Play with me?
Leave me alone.

Lexi climbs onto the windowsill and peers out between the slats in the blinds.

My phone is ringing, somewhere in this mess. Who would call at this hour? I search the floor until I find it in a jacket pocket and squint at the too bright screen. Number Withheld. I suppose it's someone chasing a bill. I blink and look again at the screen. The clock on the phone reads 18:13.

The truth of it smacks me. Like a stone casually thrown in the sea, it sinks. Another day is dead. Another dreaded night is closing in. It might engulf me now, the guilt. I feel it tugging like a current, threatening to pull me down.

I reach in my bedside drawer for a Valium strip, pop three pills on my tongue and wash them down with cherry brandy. Gulp the guilt, swallow the shame. It's not the solution, I know, but it will have to do for now. Tomorrow will be better, I'm sure. I'll begin again fresh.

Lexi is perched on the windowsill, watching the dark sky, waiting for dawn.

You can't just sit there and wait, you know. A watched kettle never rattles.

She doesn't react. Sometimes she goes into a trance. I can't reach her there. I think of the draft and want to dress her in so many jumpers, but the tension is easing in my head, in my shoulders, knees and toes until my whole self is sinking into the mattress.

Lexi's voice comes from somewhere over the hills and far away.

Are you coming back?
What sort of a question…

I hope I'm coherent. Somewhere in my mind, things are making sense. I'm walking through a meadow full of wildflowers, butterflies and bees. The trees whisper to me from a distance. Shhhh, they say, shhhh.

I tumble, weightless, into a wordless void. Today is a write-off but. Tomorrow will be better and. I'll begin again.

RUNNER-UP

ANNA DEMPSEY

This is About an Alligator and Nothing Else

Synopsis

Harley Mendoza (12) *is having the kind of summer most kids dream of. She lives in Sweetgator, Florida with her father, who she calls* **D**. *D is a single parent who loves her deeply but has struggled since Harley's mom has died because of a local factory's negligence and water poisoning. She has grown up in a quirky, plastic flamingo filled trailer park run by* ***Terry*** *which attracts tourists from all over the USA who are hoping to get a glimpse of alligators and orange groves. Her best friend* ***Rafael Padilla (12)*** *lives a few trailers down with his mother.*

The two best friends have one dream for their summer: win tickets to Magic Kingdom from a group of Christian do-gooders who visit Sweetgator every summer to help out the 'poor swamp kids'.

While Harley and Raf are at Disney World she learns that her father (D) has died of a heart attack. She goes back home and slowly falls apart now that she is orphaned with no plan moving forward. Harley desperately wants to live with Raf and his mother but soon learns this won't be a possibility due to their illegal status.

As a hurricane hits the town of Sweetgator, Harley prays for destruction so that everyone in her life can feel as broken and lost as she is. Harley gets her wish and a hurricane destroys her small town and rips her home in half. With everyone feeling a sense of loss, Raf and Harley come back together and decide to be each other's 'home'.

When Harley turns 18 she finally goes back to Sun N Fun to see her father's grave and places an orange blossom on it. At the end of the book, she can finally say the word dad again.

Where We Begin

I killed a Burmese python on my twelfth birthday.

It was the only time I ever killed a living thing on purpose. I never liked making anything die. Sure, I'd stepped on an ant before but I tried my best not to. While others poured boiling water down the ant holes, I'd jump over the dirt hills they made in the cracks of the sidewalk. And even though I hated the palmetto bugs that scurried across our bathroom floor, I wouldn't pound them with D's bug killing right shoe (never saw his left one). It didn't feel okay to kill a living thing because I knew how much it hurt for everybody left behind. The dead thing didn't care so much.

Maybe it was all the other things that happened before I killed that snake. But it's also all the things that happened after. I'm old enough now to tell the story but not so old that I'll get things wrong. I'm in a sweet spot where if I think long enough, I can remember the shelf we kept the milk with the purple cap on and the billboards that lined Main Street telling the tourists about to BOGO deals on alligator heads at the Swamp and Shop. I could tell you that the radio wouldn't stop playing Donna Lewis's 'I Love You Always Forever' and it was everybody's favorite that summer until it wasn't. If I wait any longer, those things will wash away in a thunderstorm.

Chapter 1 The midnight ride

We were looking for magic that summer. Really, we were looking for it every day down there near the swamps. Raf's eyes always on the sky trying to spot an eagle or an ibis. Mine were on the dirt, waiting for things to grow or to come back. But that June all I cared about was turning another year older and winning a pair of tickets for us to ride on Space Mountain. Things were changing quick. Coarse black hair was growing under my arms and sticking out of the sides of my underwear. I kept trying to cut it back with the kitchen scissors, but it always grew back like some well-watered crabgrass. Even the animals were changing. The manatees weren't visiting the dock as much and if they did, they weren't bringing their calves with them. But the summer couldn't officially begin till my birthday, it was like our starting pistol. Bang, here we go.

"Pedal faster, it's almost midnight," I hollered, twisting my neck to look behind me.

Raf was panting. His black bike barely visible on the dark road. Sweetgator didn't believe in having too many streetlights because of the animals and all. Didn't want to mess with the nocturnal one's like the people near the beach did. Making the mistake of leaving lights on at night which had the baby turtles hatching and walking towards what they thought was the moon reflection on the water but was just some lady's living room.

It was one of those balmy nights, the kind that left your skin sticky and let you know there'd been rain showers earlier in the day. I'd already caught a few bugs in my lip balm on the ride over, my mouth was some kind of windshield gathering up stuff. Best to keep your mouth shut though. We had all kinds of things you didn't want to swallow.

"Go on without me! Leave me here to get eaten by possums," Raf called out.

"Yeah, yeah, you know the rule. Nobody gets left behind, not even the dog."

I reached inside my back pocket to check for his inhaler doing my best to keep the bike on the yellow line that hugged the side of the road. We both carried one, just in case.

"Dolly Parton, you stay with Raf." She barked twice and ran back towards him. She was a big dog, a yellow lab or something mutt-like making it easy enough to see her in the night-time.

Raf knew he was a slow poke. He'd always get picked last in PE. Nobody did it to be a little devil to him. Matter of fact, he told them to do it. When the kids in our class tried to pick him for dodgeball or kickball or other ball stuff, he'd pretend not to hear and just stare up at the flickering lights on the gym ceiling. His bad breathing was Southern Sugar's fault. They owned most of the state. Everybody's family in Sweetgator, Belle Glade, Pahokee and anywhere near Lake Okeechobee had something. Raf's story was that he got so sick with the black smoke from all the sugar cane burns that his lungs didn't recover. I had a story too, but mine came from the ground.

My Casio watch lit up like a firefly on my wrist and read 11:52pm. I loved that thing since it was adult looking and black all over. Grabbed it from the lost and found box at Sun N Fun at the end of last summer. The light shut off meaning I'd be turning twelve soon and we needed to hurry up. The ceremony was waiting. I pushed my body forwards and pumped my legs. Raf wouldn't mind if I went up ahead. After all, it was my mom we were going to see, not his.

A coyote howled somewhere off in the scrub. I stood up on my pedals and returned its call.

"Owoooooo, ow, ow, owoooooo," I cried out, Raf and Dolly Parton joining in.

* * *

The cemetery wasn't far from where we lived at Sun N Fun. Or as Terry put on the cover of her brochures, "Your own personal paradise." People were ticked sideways when they pulled in and found a mobile home park with way too many plastic flamingos stuck in the front yards and a pool half full of algae.

Raf pulled up next to me in the gravel lot panting with sweat gathering up on his forehead. The road was silent, not a car, racoon or pick up in sight.

He reached both hands in his front and back pockets.

"Toss me the inhaler? Forgot mine."

I threw it fast in his direction. He caught it easy, shook it and sucked in a few times. Dolly Parton licked his left calf. He gave me a nod which meant he wasn't going to drop dead and we ditched our bikes against the coquina shell wall and made our way inside. The wrought-iron gate was open. It was always open. What's the point of locking them inside of there? They were all dead anyway.

"My flashlight isn't comin' on." Raf hit the blue plastic thing twice on his thigh. A light shone for a second then went off.

"That's okay, moon is plently bright. Follow me."

Dolly Parton trotted ahead towards the middle of the cemetery, the crescent sliver helping us out.

"We aren't walking on the dead are we?"

"Nah, we're all good, it's just old palm fronds," I whispered.

Raf needed me to be brave or he wouldn't do half the things I wanted. I didn't know if the dirt and the worms and all the other stuff under the ground moved and shifted. But I did know that the whole state was sinking and that our ground was wet. You could be walking to school and fall into the ground. Sinkholes were always lurking about in the ground. And that's where our water came from after all. Plenty of things were under our feet. Dead things and deadly things.

We got to her two minutes before midnight.

The dog laid down in front of the granite headstone and wrapped herself up in a loose ball. Neither of us had really known my mom. How much can a three-year-old remember? I missed her but not in a way that made me cry and wail. Sometimes I'd wake up in the middle of the night feeling like I'd forgotten something. That's what it was like.

We took turns picking the weeds and brushing away the Spanish moss that was laying around. I only came here once a year. Maybe D came more but I wasn't sure. Once I saw him, coming out of Betsy's Swamp and Shop with a bouquet of sunflowers wrapped in plastic. When he got home that night, he didn't have them. My parents were never married but they were together long enough to make a home and have a baby. Long enough to make him miss her when she died.

Raf took out a small white and red package of Little Debbie mini muffins. They were the chocolate chip kind, my favorite. He stuck a candle in one of the spongy cakes while I took out my lighter, the one we found in the teacher parking lot at school. It was purple with a naked mermaid on it.

"Want this?" Raf asked, holding out a hair band. He kept one on his wrist, the way I kept the inhaler for him. "No need to burn your hair like last year. Smelled like hell for days."

Quickly, I pulled my hair into a low pony.

The watch beeped.

"Happy birthday, Harley."

Taking a deep breath in through my nose, I made my wish. I didn't say it out loud, just in my heart or my head or wherever sad thoughts live. Then, I blew.

"Same one as last year?"

I nodded, avoiding his eyes. He always made the same mistake, thinking I'm making a wish about my Mom. But I never corrected him. That would take the magic away.

"Maybe this year the dead will rise," Raf said, touching the small golden cross that hung around his neck.

Chapter 2 Twelve

The next day was my official birthday and Dolly Parton was missing as usual so I spent my morning looking about Sun N Fun.

"Where are you, girl?" I walked slowly to the back of the house, my body aching from pedalling hard the night before. There wasn't much in the backyard but a grassy overgrown area the size of half a soccer field that led to the Pig Path. Either side of that path was full of low growing cabbage palms and mushy ground. Once you pushed passed the bushes and branches then walked a good bit you'd reach the wooden dock that jutted out into the canal. I helped D and Terry build it and rebuild it, over and over again like that. Plenty of hurricanes would take it down and I'd lost count. It was like a rainbow wooden dock with all the different planks used on it. Dolly Parton liked to laze about in a sunny spot watching the water, barking at the cranes as they guzzled fish down their skinny throats. Sweetgator had dozens of canals, needed all of them for the irrigation and of the sugarcane, peanuts, tomatoes and all. Ours was 35 ft deep and flowed right into the Loxahatchee River.

"Come on girl, don't make me search for you on my own birthday."

Nearby a robin was singing to the new day, or maybe passing along my message so my dog would listen up. Strange to hear the robin in June, should've been back up north by then.

D was taking me to Big Blue for our yearly birthday tradition of floating down the springs and eating cake. It was my favorite thing, being in the water. I loved tying the black inner tubes together with old shoelaces and gliding down the clear stream. Best part was hopping out and running back to the start to do it all over again. The whole thing took thirty minutes or about. Some kids called it the Lazy River of the South like the one up at Wet N Wild. Maybe the water wasn't heated like that place but if you were lucky you could see some tarpons and if you were double lucky, something bigger.

I had to call my dog's name three more times before she decided to care. Came darting out of those trees, tongue flapping all over.

Swap.

A screen door open and shut a few lots over where the out of towners parked their nice camper vans. It caught Dolly Parton's attention.

Standing in the doorway of the fanciest RV on the property was a boy about my age. He looked babyish wearing a matching set of black and white short sleeved Mickey Mouse pyjamas. I must have woken him up with my hollering because he was rubbing his eyes and his black hair was sticking out in all directions like a sunflower. That RV of his was huge, must've had two bedrooms in it and full kitchen and bathroom. The kid looked a little explorer, standing there peering out across the lot at the rest of Sun N Fun like it was a buffet and he was deciding if he liked what was being served or not.

"Hey there girl." The boy leaned down to tussle my dog's ears. "Where'd you come from, huh?"

Dolly Parton wagged that fluffy tail of hers and lapped it up. She didn't care one bit that he was the enemy. She liked the food and treats the random guests would sneak her and that was that. Most kids thought they'd be coming down south to go to Disney World and would end up being angry as a hive of bees when all they saw around them were swamps, fruit stands selling oranges and boiled peanuts by the sides of roads, and plenty of flying cockroaches. Lots of folks came here trying to get in touch with nature and the wild or wanted to see a "real live Indian." Now when they asked for that, Terry'd charged them more for their stay. Secretly, I think the parents hated it as much as the kids did. They all missed the AC.

"Come on girl, don't want us to leave without you do ya?" I shouted.

The boy waved but I turned away before he could say anything. Me and Raf had a rule—no making friends with the out of towners. Kids like him called Sun N Fun a trailer park, which was a dumb thing to say because it wasn't just trailers on that land. These people would come from all kinds of cities like Grand Rapids, Michigan or Sacramento, California. Places that felt fake when you said them out-loud, like they'd rumble around in your mouth like an empty dryer. Sweetgator, Florida—now that had a ring to it.

AMY ELKHEART

Manhattan Star

Synopsis

How far would you go to prevent the world from seeing who you truly are? Manhattan Star *follows the story of a young man who conceals his showgirl persona amid America's 1930 sodomy laws and Manhattan's neighbourhood gossip. It is a literary romance fiction with interwoven historical accuracies.*

Gabriel stumbles off a train in New York with nothing but his satchel and the clothes he's wearing. Out of desperation, he bags a job at Red Moon Cabaret. The twist? He is disguised each night as a showgirl, Gabriella. All seems well when the district is entranced by his act and he's earning enough money to pay for his ramshackle hotel room. That is, when he's not being harassed by Roy and the club's 'hyenas' or thinking of his missing friend, Daphne.

Everything changes when Italian café owner, Michel, moves into the building next door to the club. The pair build a tentative friendship that blossoms beyond its designed constraints. Despite Gabriel's best intentions, he falls for the Italian and Michel for 'Gabriella' in turn. Hiding the spark of romance while grappling with his past leads Gabriel to believe he can never exist unmasked. But an evening of Chianti wine leads to secrets spilled and the pair begin a terrifying, blissful relationship.

Between the bumps, troubles, and balancing acts of hiding both his identity and inclination, he discovers private Harlem gatherings that he never knew existed and with them, the return of a friend thought lost forever. Then, one small slip-up unravels Gabriel's whole world. What will happen when the district's men discover the club's coveted 'Manhattan Star' showgirl has secrets? When his existence is a matter of death or prison, how can Gabriel win? The true price of love becomes clear in a society designed to douse his flame.

ONE

Manhattan, April 1935

By day, the fabled district of Manhattan resembled any New York City neighbourhood. Businessmen strode overcrowded streets to a cacophony of shouting cab drivers. Mothers, with pinned hair and babies in arms, smiled at each other as if they didn't struggle to find coins in the dust of their purses. From morning to afternoon, a caterwaul of drills bounced between high-rise buildings as dockworkers ground down the rivets of a ship. The district itself a perfect factory of upstanding citizens, doing what they should always do and ticking over without fuss.

But Manhattan had one thing in common with the people who lived there: peel apart its layers and the truth unravels. If those mothers had searched for their lost coins outside of dusty purses, they would have been sure to find it tied up in the garters and stockings of Red Moon Cabaret. After a hard day's labour, supposedly loyal husbands joined workmen from across the city to spend their Lincolns in the bosom of frilly skirts and red lipstick.

As industry boomed and the skyline grew, so did cabaret. The more desperate workers, the more money to be made in places they frequented. Red Moon Cabaret attracted eager hordes through its crimson velvet curtains each night, where post-Prohibition whiskey coated workmen's throats and encouraged them to part with what should have belonged to their wives.

This night, like any other, was another glorious chance for patrons to indulge themselves out of their own beds. But those patrons, expecting to live out their most erotic fantasies, did not expect to see a tubby man take to the stage once again, instead of the usual dancing showgirls.

The man scraped the microphone stand across the floor and cleared his throat.

"Now, gentlemen. I know who you're here to see. The 'Manhattan Star'. Queen of Red Moon Cabaret. Here tonight, just for you fine folk." He tugged at his collar. "This dame, she's gonna drive ya wild—!"

The gentlemen he addressed – if they could be called gentlemen, smudging their whiskey glasses with stained dockworker fingers and swilling over whichever poor rhinestone waitress brought the tray – did not come to see a stout fellow with armpit sweat seeping through the lines of his tightly-buttoned waistcoat. Only the girl whose bombshell blonde hair donned half-stuck flyers on Fifth Avenue buildings and newspaper clippings across Manhattan.

"Quit yappin'!" One man booed from the crowd.

"Yeah, bring her out!"

The host gulped at the ruffled audience. He knew they would siege the stage if he kept them waiting much longer.

"One more song, she'll be out." He gestured to the saxophonist, who nodded. "One more!"

Grumbles emerged from the seats.

The man hurried behind the curtain, muttering at his timepiece.

"Annette," He called through the stagehands busying the theatre platform. "Annette!" Falling props clattered below as a girl's head poked out from the pit. A top hat sat crooked on the shiny brown hair that rested on the shoulders of her tuxedo blazer.

"Annette, where is she?"

"Don't know, Huxley."

"Better not have screwed me." He paused. "If she does come, we'll use the hoop. I need to give 'em something."

Huxley, the club manager and long-time sufferer of the men who paid his pockets, distracted himself by pacing the wing, unaware that his favourite showgirl was rushing through the walnut-grain corridors with tassels swaying against her thighs. Annette swung herself through the back curtain and listened out. Clunky heels tapped on hardwood floors, and she ran to the sound.

"Gabriella! Where've you been?"

"Those men – animals! – by the doors." Gabriella pouted, creasing her red lipstick. "He needs to do something about them. They almost ripped my garter!"

Annette sighed. "Come."

With no time for the dressing room, Annette used her fingers to fix the strays in Gabriella's hair and reattach a stocking clip that had been clawed open. She unzipped her belt bag of assorted twinkly accessories, worn by showgirls to glitter their bodices against the spotlights. There was barely time to pull on a silky glove before the show began.

Huxley had already made peace with sacrificing himself to the furious crowd as he trudged onto the stage. Before he spoke, Annette dashed to the grand piano below and winked at him. The signal that they could go ahead as planned. As Annette cracked her fingers and got ready to play, she could have sworn Huxley's knees buckled with relief.

"Here she is, here she is." Huxley may well have been reassuring himself. "Good things come to those who wait. Give a hand for the Manhattan Star, Miss Gabriella!"

The crowd howled and cheered. Ribbons fluttered down from a dangling hoop, descending. Gabriella grimaced. The hoop routine had forced the stagehands into a string of late-night rehearsals the previous week and they were supposed to have another month to perfect it. *Must be a hard crowd.* She stole a glance at Huxley before the music started. *Or a latecomer's punishment.*

A smirk replaced Gabriella's grimace. She matched Annette's upbeat piano with expected confidence. A gentle flick of the arm, seductive around the hoop. A rising leg that draped on the inner ring. Dangle it, relaxed, as if the lift doesn't nip. Ignore the harsh sandpaper grip that holds skin to hoop.

Nice and easy. Just like Daphne taught you.

The entranced audience could never have noticed such a thought process. Gabriella twirled on the ring, balancing on air and commanding it to move with grace. The bodysuit hugged her hips – a crowd favourite, no matter which girl wore it. But the stiff hemming sliced skin where thigh met waist.

Bite through it.

Gabriella's final spin spread the bodysuit's hemline tassels out, reflecting the spotlight like a ruby glittering in the sun. Cheers erupted as men clamoured over each other. They vied to be noticed by the blonde's eyes, but those eyes fixated on the spotlight. Breathing in the magic. Absorbing the heat. The only thing that mattered. The hoop jolted as Annette lowered the pulley, and Gabriella stepped onto stage at the appropriate height. One more curtsey, then raised arms. Bask in the praise, then step behind the velvet curtain.

Gabriella inhaled deeply, placing her hands on her knees to better breathe.

"Fantastic!" Annette appeared, having ran from her piano seat. "*Magnifique*! They were screamin'. That—" A red graze peeked from beneath the tassels. "You're bleeding."

"Well, beauty is pain." Gabriella nodded towards Huxley, who had plodded backstage and now made his way to the pair. "I wish he hadn't switched the schedule."

"Gabriella!" Huxley stood in front of them, cheeks rosy. "Excellent show tonight. Had the patrons swooning in their seats, you did."

"All the more to line your pockets with. But the hoop—"

"Tough crowd, see," Huxley interrupted. "Few newcomers blowin' their coin before the Radium's big show tonight. And with you being late and all, I had to make up for it."

"Blame those hyenas out front! You know the ones. Roy and his crew. They pulled me back when I tried to enter. Nearly broke my garter from grabbing. If you hadn't asked us to be nice to them, I'd have broken a glass bottle on their backs. I'm supposed to be *untouchable*."

Silence befell the three. Huxley rubbed his forehead.

"Look, my hands are tied," he said after a moment's thought. "Try not to be late again."

Gabriella and Annette watched him approach one of the more unfortunate stagehands for complaint before exhaling sighs. The pair made their way to the corridor, the club's hub for offices, storage closets, and dressing rooms.

"He'll fire me one day," Gabriella said.

"He likes you too much for that." Annette grappled with the large bundle of spare curtain in her hands, throwing it into the prop-stuffed storeroom as they walked past. "You bring in too much money for him to be angry."

The blonde swung open the door to the dressing room, chuckling. Annette followed closely, twisting the lock once she'd stepped inside.

"Let's assess the damage," Gabriella said, pulling her stocking tops off their clasps.

Annette faced the wall out of decency. Through the sound of stretching fabric, jangling beads impacting with the jewellery counter, and the tell-tale thump of a bodice landing in the corner, she listened for the splash of the basin and a scrubbing facecloth. Upon hearing the splash, she stared at Gabriella's poster until she was sure her friend had fixed whatever undergarments remained.

"Not so bad. Scrapes here, a cut there. Nothing that'll last."

Annette turned around. She looked at the figure before her, now finished inspecting skin for hoop burn. Face now absent of scarlet lipstick, bodice abandoned in the corner, and golden locks tied up to expose a lean frame covered with only the necessary accoutrements.

Sometimes, even Annette forgot.

"Yeah, could be worse… Gabriel."

TWO

Manhattan, the year before

A steam train rolled into Manhattan's 125th St station, where overcast skies broke to reveal a skim of sun on New York's high-rise buildings. A young man scrambled to the train doors as they clanged open, uttering apologies to any disgruntled passengers he squeezed past. He stepped onto the brickwork platform, finding the city air preferable to the stuffy cabin swelter he'd endured on his ride from Chestertown.

The young man looked at his ticket, which he had wrapped in his identity card for fear of being thrown off the train should he lose it.

Gabriel Abraham Walker. He ran his finger across the indent of the name. *Not anymore.*

Billowing steam pulled his attention away from the passport. He lifted his satchel strap to free his stuck plait. Gabriel liked length in his hair, but conceded to the plait a few years before. He could hide it in the tuck of his shirt, and if he greased his scalp with pomade like those men on billboards did, no one would be wise to it. Anything to stop his father lunging at him with scissors to cut it all off.

He considered himself fortunate to have arrived in New York without a slew of luggage. He had grabbed his small satchel between screams as he rushed out the door of his father's house, wearing only the clothes on his back. Inside the satchel, he had been grateful to find a small notebook and enough money from his job at the greengrocers to catch a train out of Chestertown. At least such a slim amount of property wouldn't burden him on his way through the city streets.

And those streets, he realised, were vast. Spreading in straight, square webs through the skyscrapers. He gawked up at the tall buildings until his eyes slipped back to his feet from nausea. Chestertown's tiny, grass-tufted lanes and porch rocking chairs seemed an impossible memory here. No cicada to chirrup the morning in, and no church-goers gripping rosary beads between white knuckles. It didn't look like anyone prayed here.

Gabriel preferred that.

Coming to terms with his surroundings was no easy feat. He tailed behind the crowds marching across cracked pavements, finding himself elbowed and bumped by passers-by until he managed to fall into rhythm. After an hour of navigating the colossal city, he dove down a side street and drew in a breath.

A passing car blared as his foot shot back onto the kerb. He cracked his back to relieve the ache of his walking and observed his surroundings. Populated, but with enough space to stretch in. New York's frantic bustle echoed from behind, muffled by the barrier of buildings that separated countless frowning businessmen from the avenue's leisurely retirement.

He looked to the left. A peeling sign creaked on its hinges. 'VACANCIES'. The lodging's masonry seemed like it would fall apart if he tugged the door. Gabriel opened his satchel and counted the change inside. Just enough for one night, with a few dimes on top.

He wiped his head as he entered to make sure no rubble had dusted him. Cigarette smoke clung to the curtains and the floorboards felt like sponge beneath his feet. At the desk, an old woman with grey curls and thick glasses sifted through papers.

"Hello, I'd like a room please." Gabriel said. The old woman put her finger up as if rejecting the interruption. He stood in an awkward stance until she had sorted whatever she was working on in her ledger.

"Cash." She held out her hand.

On giving up his change, the old woman handed him a stained key with a card that read 'Room 15'. The staircase creaked as he ascended. He nudged open the door, finding a plain bed, a lamp, a full-length mirror, and a wooden wardrobe inside.

Not bad. No rats nibbling the wall skirting. No bloodstained duvets from a recent murder. He sat on the edge of the mattress, digesting the day. He put down his satchel, loosened his suspenders, and unbuttoned his shirt.

The mirror left no part of him unexposed. He stared at himself. His fingers ghosted across his bruises as if they might burn him. Purple welts, embedded in his skin by slashing leather, bloomed out into greyish yellow. He had not been privileged enough to leave that house without one more beating.

He pressed gently on one of the welts, then turned to inspect his back as best he could. The whip of his father's belt had imprinted lines down the side he could see. He winced at the memory.

"Sodomy! Fornication!" His father had yelled, each word staccato with the slashes.

It had been quick. An experiment. The boy ran errands part-time at the greengrocers where Gabriel worked and they talked now and then. They were the same age. Forming a friendship was only natural.

"You're like me, aren't ya?" The boy had said once, picking up a delivery of strawberries.

Gabriel hadn't responded. But the day before the altercation with his father, the boy kissed him behind the park shed. It was an unexceptional moment. They weren't in love. Sparks didn't fly when they touched, and the only magical thing they saw in each other's eyes was understanding. But he felt more towards that boy than for any girl that his friends had ever fancied.

I think I am.

A neighbour had spotted them. That neighbour complained to the greengrocer because he refused to buy food touched by a faggot. The greengrocer called to the house and brought a torrent down on Gabriel's father for raising such a son. And no sooner had the porch door closed, his father had pounded up the stairs, dragged eavesdropping Gabriel back from his escape out the bedroom window, and beat him inconsolable on the hardwood floor.

E. H. EWART

The Pope is Dead

Synopsis

The Pope is Dead *is a novel about an art historian with a troubled past and the artist whose work he most admires but whose character he finds disturbingly flawed. It is a novel about love, friendship, loss, the inability to do the right thing at the right time, the resultant guilt, and the deeply wished for but non-existent connection between great art and morality. It is in three parts, set in three locations, and spans three decades. Each part begins with the announcement of the death of a pope.*

Le Pape est Mort: On the day Pope Paul VI dies, Hugh Murray, a Canadian PhD candidate at Columbia University and his wife, Vera, arrive in Quebec to spend a few quiet weeks at the summer home of Luc Lacroix, an artist whose paintings are the subject of Hugh's dissertation. They expect to be alone with Luc but find themselves in the midst of his fiercely unwelcoming family. As Hugh settles down to write, Vera is on the front line of the family's hostility. One morning, Hugh and Vera witness an incident between Luc and his daughter, Axelle. Vera is convinced that the girl is being sexually abused, but Hugh is unwilling to acknowledge it.

The Pope is Dead: Back in New York, Vera is still deeply troubled by her experiences in Quebec. She loathes Luc and grows increasingly resentful of Hugh's blindness.

De Paus is Dood: Hugh, now a professor at NYU, is on sabbatical at Ghent University. Vera is divorcing him. As his father lay dying, he had warned Hugh that there is a day in everyone's life when they realize they are all they ever will be. Hugh had assumed that his father was speaking of accomplishments but finally realizes that he was referring to character.

THE POPE IS DEAD

ONE

August 6, 1978

Le Pape est mort.

I didn't catch the first part of the sentence, "*Who* died?"

"Le Pape – the Pope," Luc leaned over and turned up the car radio to listen to the details. When the announcement was over, he switched it off, "Eymard is going to be upset."

"Eymard?"

"My sister-in-law – Sister Eymard."

"Is she a nun, an actual nun?"

"Oui," Luc said. "She's a missionary. Bernadette's bringing her up to the cottage tomorrow. It's the first time she's been home in twenty years."

And the Pope has to die when she's here. That's too bad. But how the hell am I supposed to get any work done with so many people around? I was there to work on my dissertation on Luc's paintings. Because he had a summer studio at Lac Foncé, a small lake two hours from Montreal, he'd suggested it might be interesting if my wife and I stayed at his cottage for a month, or longer if necessary. That way, I could see his new work and write without the usual distractions. I had jumped at the chance. My mother-in-law had recently passed away, and my wife was in need of a rest, so the prospect of a few quiet weeks at a lake in Quebec was something I couldn't turn down. Besides, it had been an unusually hot July, and Vera and I were thrilled to get out of New York for the rest of the summer.

* * *

We had flown into Dorval Airport earlier that morning, and I showed Vera the wall where Greg Curnoe's mural had hung for a short time before it was taken down and shipped to the National Gallery in Ottawa.

"Why would they commission it and then remove it?" she asked.

"There was a problem with one of the figures in the painting. Greg depicted a friend of his named Jack Kelly being mutilated by the propeller of a zeppelin."

"Yikes! Not the best subject for an airport."

"That's not why they took it down. The real reason was that Jack Kelly bore a striking resemblance to Lyndon Johnson."

* * *

Luc met us at Dorval and said he had to stop at his house to pick up a few things to take to the cottage.

It was Vera's first time in Montreal, and she was excited when we began to ascend Mont Royal.

"This is Westmount," Luc said. "When I was a boy, this area was all English. There wasn't one Québécois living here. Now there are at least a dozen families." As we drove up the mountain, the houses became larger and more impressive as brick gave way to stone. "Things change. It takes time, but sooner or later everything changes," Luc pulled into a wide crushed-brick driveway.

The house, like everything I associated with Luc or would ever associate with Luc, was grand. But there was a funny smell about the place – a bad smell – as though it hadn't been lived in for a couple of weeks, and someone had left an open bag of garbage under the sink.

Apart from his own work and the work of a couple of Canadian artists he admired, Luc had an impressive collection of American art.

I was staring at a Hans Hoffman when he walked up behind me, "Beautiful, eh?"

"It's one of the best Hoffman's I've ever seen."

"It's damaged," he pointed to the bottom of the painting, "right there."

I looked closely. I could see a small area where the paint had been retouched. "Was it like that when you bought it?"

"No, it was perfect when I bought it. It was stolen from this house a few years ago. The police found it in a ditch three weeks later."

Vera was staring at the damage, too, "Why would anyone go to the trouble of stealing a painting only to dump it in a ditch?"

"They were Axelle's friends."

"Axelle?" she said.

"My daughter."

I could see the shocked expression on Vera's face. She told me later that I'd looked pretty shocked myself.

"She gave the house keys to some friends of hers," Luc said, "and told them what to take – what jewellery, what paintings. They only took the most valuable stuff, and the police didn't find everything. My Order of Canada medal and a lot of jewellery that belonged to Bernadette's mother are still missing, but we got all the paintings back."

"Why would she do a thing like that – have you robbed?" Vera asked.

"It was four years ago," Luc said, as though that explained it. "She was only thirteen."

I felt it best to leave the conversation there, "This is a very special

Hoffman and an excellent restoration job. I wouldn't have noticed it was damaged if you hadn't pointed it out."

"That's good to hear, but, for me, it's the first thing I see when I look at it now." Luc disappeared into the kitchen, *"Axelle will be at the lake, too!"*

"That's something to look forward to," Vera whispered in my ear.

"With her boyfriend!" Luc added.

"Great!" I shouted to Luc and began counting bodies – Luc, Bernadette and her sister, Axelle and a boyfriend, Vera and me, and Luc had mentioned earlier that his son would be there as well.

Luc appeared in the doorway carrying a cardboard box filled with bags of flour, some canned goods, paper napkins, and a couple of flashlights, "She comes up every weekend with her boyfriend, but they don't stay at the cottage. They have a tent in the woods."

* * *

On the way to the cottage, I learned a lot about Luc I hadn't known before. He was one of twelve children, the youngest of seven brothers. Being an only child, I'd often wondered about such large families, and I could hear my mother say disdainfully, "They wouldn't be able to remember each other's names!" They weren't a close family. Luc never saw most of them, just two younger sisters who idolized him. One was a librarian who, from Luc's description, sounded a bit mannish; the other was a schoolteacher who was married to Luc's barber, although judging from the length of Luc's hair, he couldn't have seen them too often either. The rest of the family were festering with jealousy and hitting him up for money every time they got together, so he'd cut them out of his life years ago. One brother had recently attempted a reunion, but it hadn't gone well.

"Tabernac!" Luc said, at the thought of it. "You have to have something to speak about when you speak. Oui? Otherwise, it's a waste of time."

Somehow or other, after an hour on the road, we got around to the topic of death. I glanced at Vera, who was in the back seat. She hadn't spoken for a while, and I was relieved to see that she had dozed off. Luc had an idea that he elaborated on for several miles. I don't know whether it was the piety surrounding funerals that turned his stomach or if he was just excited by the novelty of his own thought, but he felt that most people were "poseurs" and since they went through life presenting a certain ridiculous, pretentious face to the world, that's exactly how they should be buried. Instead of being laid to rest stretched out in hypocritical peacefulness with a rosary in their hands, they should be arranged in their most arrogant pose and preserved in a transparent block of plastic, like a fly in an ice cube. Then he'd shout out the name of a critic or curator we both knew and screw that magnificent face of his into an uncanny, sneering, pompous likeness of them, which he'd hold for a moment before collapsing with laughter over the steering wheel. Luc went on and on with one example after another, perhaps too long, but his laughter was infectious, and I was just happy to be there, driving through the Quebec countryside with Canada's greatest artist. The next time I checked on Vera, she was still asleep.

"I'm grateful for the opportunity to write at your cottage," I said.

"You'll be alone at the cottage most of the time. Right now, I'm working on a new series of paintings in Montreal. I'll stay for a few days on this trip, but after that, I'll only see you on the weekends. I'll give you Camille's phone number if you need to contact me. I'm usually at her place after six."

I'd met Camille, Luc's present mistress, on a former trip to Montreal. She was an art student in her second year at the university. Beautiful, moody, and cunning.

"Bernadette doesn't come to the cottage very often. You'll probably see Fabien more than anyone, but he's very quiet. He likes to sail. And Axelle – well, that's hard to say – she comes and goes as she pleases," he made a large sweeping gesture with his hand, "Comme le vent. The wind – like the wind. She is a force of nature. You might see her several times a day or not at all, but she never sleeps at the cottage in the summer."

I could smell water in the air as we neared the lake. I'm very good at that. I grew up on Lake Ontario, and I can always pick up the scent of water miles before anyone else can. That's why I like living in Manhattan. I love that distinct smell of water that hangs over the island, which most people don't even notice.

There had been, as Luc put it, "some slight damage" to the property when he'd bought it. The thought came over me that a lot of things in Luc's life were damaged, but perhaps that's the nature of genius – the ability to form some surprisingly marvellous order out of chaos. We finally turned off the main road onto a narrower road. It was perfectly paved and seemed especially long and circuitous. I had expected it to branch off to other cottages, but it never did. It was a direct route to Luc's summer home – a private road that wound through a dense wood flickering with sunlight. As we neared the cottage, Luc explained how the previous owner, the heir apparent to one of Montreal's major crime families, had met with an 'accident' when he'd stepped into his car one July morning after a weekend of fishing at the lake. The repairs Luc had to make amounted to filling in a crater and resurfacing the driveway, but, except for that, everything was perfect. At least that's how he saw it.

* * *

"Perfect, eh!" Luc said as we stepped into the sprawling summer home. After setting the cardboard box down on the marble counter, which divided the kitchen from the living room, he held his arms out and turned full circle, "It came furnished, and we didn't have to change a thing!"

He looked around for his son, *"Fabien!"*

There was no answer.

The cottage was more like a house. In fact, it was an extremely large house, a two-story yellow brick house. Everything was very well made, very expensive, and in very bad taste. It was so well insulated that it was cool indoors even though it was a stiflingly hot day.

"It's beautiful in the wintertime, too," Luc said when he saw Vera looking at the oversized fieldstone fireplace in the living room. "The lake freezes over every winter, and if the roads are clear, we sometimes come here to skate on the weekends. We even spent last Christmas here."

Luc led us upstairs to the room that would be ours for the next few weeks. It was at the back of the house and was much bigger than we had expected. There was a large en-suite bathroom and a walk-in closet.

When we were finally alone, Vera ran around examining everything, "I can't believe the size of this room, and we've got our own bathroom! It's like a fancy hotel!"

So, this is where I'll work on my doctoral dissertation, I thought, as I stared at a swivel chair and a wooden table that would serve as my desk. Remarkable for their simplicity, they looked out of place. Another thing that looked out of place was the bookcase. Luc had told me that he would provide me with all of his catalogues, and there they were, arranged in chronological order on the shelves.

Our bedroom windows overlooked the roof of Luc's studio, which was a two thousand square foot rectangular addition to the house. A skylight ran the full length of it, but at such an angle that it was impossible to see inside. Beyond that was a forest.

As we freshened up, Vera began complaining that there was no hypoallergenic soap in the bathroom, "What's wrong with people anyway? Why do they always buy scented soap?"

"They probably like the way it smells," I suggested.

"My eczema will flare up if I use that soap!"

"You knew you'd need special soap, so why didn't you bring some with you?"

"I thought I did, but it's not in my suitcase," she sat down on the bed, looking grim. "The last town we passed is only about five miles from here. Maybe Luc could take us there to get some?"

"Now?"

"Of course, now."

"Are you out of your mind? I'm not going to ask Luc Lacroix to go shopping for soap after he's been driving for two hours! Besides, it's Sunday – nothing's open."

"There's usually one drugstore open on Sundays, and it's not like Luc's tired or anything."

"We're in rural Quebec, Vera! And it's not a matter of life and death, so you'll have to wait until tomorrow."

When we stopped arguing, we walked down the elaborately carved oak staircase, which gently spiralled to the living room.

* * *

We found Luc on the patio with his eyes shut. He looked up when he heard the sliding door. Three tall glasses of lemonade with ice cubes and sprigs of fresh mint were sweating on the table in front of him. He motioned for us to help ourselves, "How do you like your room?"

"It's sensational!" Vera said.

"And a perfect place to write," I added.

"It's the most isolated room in the house. Very quiet. You can't hear anything when the door's closed, and there's a beautiful view of the woods and my atelier, so you won't forget why you're here!"

"There's not much chance of that," I said. "Do you have any new paintings?"

"There's always something new. If I don't work every day, my head starts to ache." He stared at the sky, "I'll show you some things tomorrow at noon, when the light's perfect."

MARIE GETHINS

The Perpetual Lives of Horace Greenly

Synopsis

Missing his left calf from birth and living adulthood for the twentieth time in Victorian London, ***Horace Greenly*** *is frustrated. For no matter his actions or choices, death is always temporary. As a solitary immortal he witnesses change, or the lack of it, haunted by voices from the past. Nothing disturbs this pattern until now. Just as he finds a way to improve the lives of other physically disabled, a mysterious Egyptian woman appears, not only threatening his plans in this life, but potentially altering the world for eternity.*

The Perpetual Lives of Horace Greenly *follows Ancient Roman Horace through three time periods: Victorian London, 1985-1987 San Francisco Bay Area, and 2055-2056 Stockholm. As he works to effect positive change through the eras, the other immortal makes sinister plans. They play a moral game of chess across time and geography. In a futuristic Stockholm, Horace faces two penultimate options: achieve death's release through medical innovation or remain to thwart a future he cannot allow.*

LONDON 1866

I

A Sunday at the London Zoological Gardens in 1866

At the ornate gates I show my annual subscription card to the ticket inspector. He forces a handbill touting the various exhibits into my palm: Old Martin the Grizzly Bear, Obaysch the Hippopotamus—a gift from the Ottoman Viceroy. 'FIRST SEEN IN EUROPE SINCE THE ROMAN EMPIRE.'

Incorrect, but I will not enlighten them. This, my twentieth adult life, brings amusement and tedium in equal measure.

I reach the wolf enclosure and settle upon a bench. The alpha stops at iron railings, his amber eyes reach inside my chest, tug my accelerated heart. We are old friends. However, my pulse doesn't race for him. A memory of his ancestor sets its rapid tempo.

Wild beasts provide fleeting tremors. Man's folly is the true implement of destruction. I have witnessed such. Wandering for more than two millennia, my uneven gait crossing the Continent. From Rome's glory to debauched abyss, onwards through shifting kingdoms and empires, I alone a perpetual spectator of his capacity for brutality. Caught in this infernal cycle of regeneration, forced to live my adult years anew, lassitude pervades me now. And yet, there is no recourse.

'Why don't his shoes match?' A girl in a tweed coat with a velvet collar and button boots stands before me, pointing at my false leg. An elegant woman, two spots colouring her cheeks, addresses me: 'I am dreadfully sorry.' She drags the girl away. A familiar smell drifts across my face. A keeper is tossing purple horsemeat to the pack. An excited crowd forms to block my view.

I stand, grimace as the stump adjusts into the prosthesis socket. This sham limb is much lighter than my ancient original. Mother paid dearly for it: carved wood wrapped in bronze, the inert calf muscles artistically executed. I dragged the device like an anchor and left a channel in the dust behind me. With the current model's springs and pivot joints, I can mimic perambulation for a time. But now, I am weary. A hansom cab to my ground floor rooms. Mrs Barnett will have a plate of cold beef and sharp cheddar waiting. Perhaps currant cake or jam roly-poly for pudding. 'You need feeding up, Mr Greenly, what with the week of work ahead.' Her Sunday refrain.

Rutledge Translation Office, later that week

Solus. Merely a Latin word on this ancient page, the religious musings of an early Christian, but it sounds in my head as a command. A voice full of gravel and spit. Not the Celtic monk, but my tutor in his purple-edged toga, chastising me.

I pinch the top of my nose, loosen the knot of my linen cravat, take measured breaths. The Tower at Westminster chimes three. Its Great Bell marking hours these past seven years—a sliver of my existence. Yet, the fishnet weave of the tutor's sandals continues to bind my thoughts. I am a youth searching the mosaic floor for a response. The tutor's hand forces my chin up. His breath, full of garlic and rotting teeth, rolls over me. I stare at his froth of silver nasal hair.

'Sir, the page.'

An urgent whisper from John Gardner, the office boy, dispels the vision. I smile at his lowered eyebrows, follow the length of his arm to a grimy finger indicating the ink blotch. He worries for me, imagines docked pay.

I wink at him, crumple the spoiled sheet and pull a new one from under my desk. He shakes his head, takes the paper ball, adds it to the smouldering fire. On Saturday evening, my paymaster, Obadiah Rutledge, will make his reckoning. Round as a melon, he fills this tiny sanctuary. All bluster of aristocratic dinner engagements and *soirées*—I alone responsible for his tardiness—he will count the pages of translation, gauge them against the unblemished sheaf, subtract those that I have wasted. No one grasps purse strings tighter, but Rutledge knows he will not find a swifter or more accurate translator. A click of the tongue is the only censure he will dare.

'More coal on the fire, John. My blood is turning to ice.'

The boy frowns, this time at my extravagance. The elbow-patches on his chestnut jacket and lines of wear above the hem of his trousers reveal extended use. He adds two small lumps to the grate.

'Come now, build it up properly. I think we've earned a dish of tea.'

I swing off the high stool, grab the desk for balance. John drops the fire tongs and hurries to my weak side. Together we hobble to the coatrack, and I explore the pockets of my herringbone Ulster. I hand him a waxed-paper parcel.

'Gingerbread.'

'Thank you, sir.' His lips quiver.

'Well, get going, man! Stoke up the fire. Hang the kettle.'

He helps me reach the ladder-back chair by the hearth and sets to work. The promise of a treat speeds his movements. A good lad. The familiar tingling starts along my scalp, travels down arms, torso, thighs. A wave of pain rocks my stump.

Insipiens. UNWISE.

A multitude of faces appear in the shadows. Mother, aunts, cousins, friends, lovers. They shout the same message in Latin, Greek, Saxon, Middle English, Dutch, Irish, Old French, Armenian.

Insipiens. UNWISE.

A strident voice cuts through, silences the rest. *Imprudentis condulcabitur*. Of course, Mother. Giulia the Vigilant. Or should I say Virginal? She should have been Cassandra, always predicting doom. She's a gnat buzzing in my ear. I close my eyes, resolve to complete our mental conversation.

Mother, back from the dead—again.

No attachments. You know this, Horatius.

He's just a boy. What harm? I will never have one of my own.

He could destroy you.

If only it could be so.

This must cease.

A rumble in my throat. Forever the same, Mother: s*olus, sola, solum.*

The rattle of a china cup and saucer. I open my eyes.

'Here, sir.' John places a plate of gingerbread on my lap and offers a chipped, rose-trimmed cup. 'It's good and strong.'

'Strong enough to trot a mouse across it?'

He laughs. 'No doubt and two spoons of sugar, as you like.'

Insipiens. UNWISE.

'Enough.' I wave my free hand, swatting her away.

'Sir?'

'Two spoons—sweet *enough* for anyone, wouldn't you say?'

Lazy smoke drifts up from the hissing grate, coals glow orange. John sits on a low stool, dampening a finger to pick up crumbs. I offer my portion of gingerbread. He hesitates before accepting. We are comfortable in silence. The previous office boy chatted from morning light until the candles burned low. A relief when Rutledge moved him to the shop and publishing house on The Strand. Once, after a particularly loud week, I told Rutledge there was no need for an office boy here. I work best alone. He coughed, muttered about my 'infirmity,' hastened to his carriage.

For a year, perhaps a bit more, John and I have shared this small room. My desk, two chairs at the hearth, a low stool, several cabinets—the boy keeps all in good order. Bookshelves cover one wall, filled with reference texts in languages of this world and long ago. He dusts spines to maintain the gold-lettering glimmer. A display for non-existent visitors.

He hovers, ready to pour tea. Another cup and I'd have to call for the piss pot—an event I try to limit to once a day in the boy's presence. 'No, mustn't waste the light,' I say. He sets the teapot on his stool and helps me to my desk. Despite our familiarity, the boy's strength is a surprise each journey we take across this room. Gaunt and introspective, he seems a fragile moth.

'Perhaps your pen needs washing?' John tugs at my arm, shifts it away from the page as another ink-drop falls. Harmless this time, onto the desk blotter. The boy dabs it with a rag. I hand him my clean pen. He strokes the bone handle's intricate carvings, traces the metal checkerboard down to the nib. He carries the pen to a bowl like an offering, plunges his rag into water and begins a delicate rub.

John returns my pen. I dip and finish the monk's sentence. *God is my protector*. My snort raises a quizzical look, but I press on until a neck cramp cannot be ignored. The boy has lit candles. Outside, lamplighters exchange jovial calls and miniature suns appear, casting a row of hazy skirts onto the footpath. Bodies pass by the windows, silhouettes between luminous puddles. Above, flues belch clouds from newly lit fires until combined with Thames' fog, they descend as brackish mist. Fingers of this gloom creep between the window transom to reach inside my throat.

I cough into my handkerchief and fold away the grey globule. A harbinger of death for many, but not for me.

'It must be past your time, John. Off with you.'

'Shall I help you with the leg before I go?'

I nod, and he brings over my latest monstrosity purchased from Cork Street. Its mechanics dazzle the boy: an ivory ankle ball in a vulcanized rubber socket, the steel bone running up the centre, and the entire false limb encased in leather to be laced on like a boot. A novelty. He is more accustomed to sailors and soldiers tapping about on peglegs near the quays. I grimace as he tightens the straps onto my left stump. He stops, but I motion for him to continue.

'I could wait, help you home. It'll be no trouble,' John says.

'It is a brief cab ride to Manchester Square and your mother is waiting.'

He cocoons his neck in a black knitted scarf, pulls on mittens. I swivel on the stool and search for my place in the text.

'Sir?' John loiters by the door. 'The carvings on your pen. Why is the snake eating its own tail?'

'Ouroboros, almost as old as time itself.' I smile. 'Some believe the Egyptians created the figure, others believe it is even older. It symbolises the cycle of Nature—creation from destruction, life comes from death. The snake eats its own tail to survive, an eternal cycle of renewal.' I lean across the desk, lower my tone. 'The Greeks used it for magic.'

'My mother says, "No such thing."' John shrugs. 'Good night, sir.' He closes the door with a soft click.

Onyx eyes peer from the top of the pen. I run a finger along its ivory scales, tail to head. I savour the shiver it sends along my arm and return to the lonely monk's pages.

II

Another Sunday visit to the London Zoological Gardens in 1866

The horse's hooves strike cobblestones while my cab's clockwork taximeter ratchets up the fare. John would hang his head through the window to watch the numbers mount. It is unlikely he will ever enter a hansom. Perhaps he might spend his free day with me. He has his family, of course, but I could make a case. As his mentor, I offer the chance to rise above his current circumstance. No doubt he'd prefer the mechanics of the Underground Metropolitan Railway. 'They say Paddington to Farringdon in eighteen minutes, sir! Colossal speed.'

Colossal—a word scrap, one of the many that he gathers from our conversations to later test upon me. The newspapers talk of noxious fumes and crowds lingering in London's bowels. Passengers wait on platforms as still as the Greek Colossus, but of ordinary stature. Could we venture it during a quiet period? It would delight the boy obsessed with industrial progress. No. Even with John's help the stairs would be insurmountable.

The hansom jolts. My stump end slams into the metal cup, pain sears along the bone up to my hip. 'Sorry, sir. It's heaving. All the world is out on God's day.' The driver shifts on his high perch. I peer around his posterior—endless immobile carriages line the Outer Circle. Although the Zoological Gardens are a fair distance, I will make better time on foot. A tap of my brass-headed cane stops the meter. Fare paid, I hobble down the two steps.

Already the paths are full of walkers. Sunday—*dies solis*—the day of rest when London's bon-ton parade their finery in The Regent's Park. In my narrow-check trousers, cream waistcoat and silk ascot, I am no different. It is the day of my greatest exertion. Even after centuries of practice, I am unable to hide my unwieldy gait. Sympathetic smiles greet me. They assume Crimean War veteran. My Savile Row tailor declares 'a well-cut suit defines a man.' However, in John's East End, even this attire would not save my stump from curled lips. An intact man holds singular value for the lower class. The boy alone does not look upon my limp with pity or indifference.

Sun fingers poke through clouds to warm my back. I snatch bits of conversations: a cook over-salting last night's turtle bisque, a footman who ill-pressed his master's Friday copy of *The Times*, two haw-haw swells plotting subterfuge to poach Lord C's valet.

'Horace?'

Rutledge approaches, with a thickset woman in a cascade of frills clinging to his arm. As if giants rolled them in a game of boules, they careen down the wide lane and block my path.

'My, my! How unusual to see you here,' he says.

I meet his stare. His eyebrows rise, disappearing into the crown of his top hat. I angle towards his companion.

'O yes, my lady wife, Annabelle.'

We exchange nods.

'Looking quite smart, Greenly.' Pounds, shillings, and pence total in my employer's pupils as he surveys my ensemble.

I lean into his ear. 'A valet friend. His master's castoffs. Alas my friend's height and girth prevents him from making use of them.'

'A stout valet? Rare.' He waves a hand from my shoulder-to-feet like a street peddler. 'All in the latest mode. His master is generous indeed. And a perfect fit. How fortunate for you.'

Rutledge waggles his chin. I smile but utter no response. Mrs Rutledge clears her throat, tugs her husband's elbow. She tilts, eyes indicating my false leg. Obadiah shakes his head. She frowns at her husband, smiles at me.

'Mr Greenly, so brave,' she says. 'The ladies of our guild…'

He interrupts. 'Well, we must make haste. Taking tea at the Trollopes'.'

I tip my bowler. Rutledge frowns as if he has discovered a spoiled egg. His wife tosses a final look over her shoulder as he pulls her down the lane. The pair waddle in the direction of Mayfair, while I continue my slow progress to the Zoological Gardens.

I take my weekly position at the wolf enclosure. The alpha pauses to meet my eyes before continuing his circuit along the iron railings. I pull a notebook and pencil from my pocket, beginning to sketch. A portrait first, but the scene shifts—cage bars melt into pines, grass springs from the concrete floor. On another *dies solis*, in another land, my father, the master of stealth, is pulling me from my bed at twilight, unbeknownst to my uncle or mother. He lifts me onto a slave's back. 'You should have made this journey long ago,' my father says. 'Remember it.'

HIGHLY COMMENDED

ALISON THERESA GIBSON

Bound in Shallows

Synopsis

Pearl, her husband Flannery, and their girlfriend Isla, have survived the catastrophically high sea levels together on their boat. They eat basic foodstuffs. Their neighbours, who disapprove of their living situation, keep their distance. Pearl is happy with her unorthodox, satisfying, arrangement. Except now, as land begins to appear again, a question is raised about what a return to normal will mean for them.

Into this situation arrives Scott, Isla's brother. He needs somewhere to stay since the government has commandeered his land. Although the rhythm on the boat is disturbed, Pearl enjoys his company. Perhaps, a little too much. Nothing, however, compares to the coming disruption.

Despite a mutual agreement to not bring a child into the world, Isla falls pregnant. Pearl is distraught at the thought of both raising a child in extreme uncertainty, and not being a biological parent to 'their' child. Isla, however, is determined. They find a new balance, and prepare for life as parents, buoyed by the hope that the sea levels are falling.

As more land appears, however, the government grows concerned over its limited resources and starts enforcing controls per 'family'. The situation forces the three to ask the question: who is the legal family in their arrangement, and how will the baby change that?

When Isla falls ill, the throuple, and Scott, head inland to find her urgent medical attention. The medical establishment is not used to coping with three parents, and when the stress causes cracks in their intimacies, Pearl seeks solace with Scott. It is a flimsy plaster on her problems, however, and Pearl realises the question is not what happens to her loved ones if the world returns to normal. The question is, is living a socially accepted existence worth giving up the people you love?

Part one

Dark water slipped down the wooden walls. We would need to sort that out in the morning. Wood creaked under my feet. My life, in its entirety, was made up of wood and water.

The bed was the one thing that didn't creak when it moved. Flannery made sure of that. I could see the curve of his body under the sheet, leaving room for a body to curl into him. I wouldn't presume that he only thought of it as my body, but for tonight it would be.

He was silent as I slipped under the sheet, but his fingers drifted up my bare arm, before he wrapped himself around me. His breath was on my neck before I felt him drifting back into sleep. His arm grew heavy around me, his breathing deepened. I knew I would have to wait for the morning, it was how he operated. Right now, his thoughts were laced with whiskey, his bones heavy from a day of trying to keep us alive. In the morning, he would be filled with the energy of a new day.

* * *

The sunlight was still an hour away when I felt him stir. He drew his hand up my arm, my skin turning to goosebumps under his touch, and let it stroke my neck, my throat, my lips. I knew he was checking that I was who he thought I was, but I didn't mind. I bit his finger, and felt his breath stop in his lungs, pressed to my back. I let my tongue follow the curve of his knuckle until I knew he was awake.

Isla eyed us as we emerged for breakfast. She smiled when he pulled his jumper over his head, rumpling his hair. We each kissed her, as we did every morning. She smelled like sour mornings, I smelled like him. She was making coffee, and poured me a cup. I didn't want to drink it, I wanted to keep that lingering taste of him, but I accepted it anyway. That was our arrangement.

'I'm going to seal that leak this morning,' Isla said. Flannery caught my eye.

'I'll help,' I said.

* * *

I had twelve hundred jars of insects when I was growing up. Not all at the same time, but over the years. I started the collection with my uncle when I was six, and a ladybird crawled across my pillow when he was putting me to bed. I wanted her to still be there when I woke up in the morning, so he found an old mustard jar and scooped her into it for me.

I wonder where those jars are now. I imagine them bobbing in the sea, spread throughout the world. Maybe someone on another boat will fish one out of the water and keep it by their bed. The crusted remains of an insect can be surprisingly good company.

* * *

Dinner was fish and potatoes with the rotten parts cut out. They were delicious, mainly due to the honey Flannery had managed to bring back. We didn't ask how he paid for it, we knew, and he knew we knew. We left him alone that night, as per our agreement.

'You still smell like sealant,' Isla said as we lay in bed. She held my fingers to her nose. Her breath was soft on my skin.

'I washed,' I said.

'I know, I'm not complaining.' She kissed my fingers, one at a time. 'How long do you think it will last this time?' she asked. I didn't know why she asked when she knew the answer. Maybe we were running out of things to say to each other.

'Until the next storm,' I said.

She placed my hand against the warm base of her neck, and turned her head to look out the small window. The air was muggy, it was always muggy.

'Ten days,' she said.

'Fourteen.'

When she looked at me, the light glinted in her eyes.

'We'll get his bet in the morning.'

I knew she was still awake as I drifted to sleep. She never slept long enough to let the dreams start.

* * *

Mum taught me to swim before I could walk, but her knowledge of swimming was limited to floating on her back, and doing a slow breaststroke with her head above the water. She was languorous, and didn't understand that sometimes there might be a need for speed in the water. Our first lesson, she held me as I floated on my back, and the chlorinated water licked the sides of my head. My ears were covered so I couldn't hear what she said, but her mouth was moving. Her eyes were bright. They were always bright in the water.

* * *

I was up early in the morning. The clouds were heavy, proving both mine and Isla's predictions of the next storm's arrival wrong. We were always wrong. We always hoped it would be weeks away, when in reality it had never been more than six days between washouts. Not for decades.

I stood outside, watching the sun create a halo from behind the clouds. The air was thick with moisture and my skin was damp, whether with sweat or simply from the air, I no longer had any idea. Our mooring was stable, the land on one side a constant mirror of the horizon on the other, and yet so often I felt like the view was changing. Some days the sea was like shards of ice, harsh and violent, and some days it was too bloated to move in anything but languorous swells. This morning it was bloated, and I watched the boats of our neighbours rise and fall gently against their moorings. Everything was silent but for the lapping water again the thick mud of the shore. There was a figure moving outside on the furthest boat, but we didn't acknowledge each other. They never acknowledged us. Our arrangement was to no one's liking but our own, and it kept them all at a distance. Isla didn't mind, she craved only the company of Flannery and me. Sometimes, I would have liked to be able to visit someone for a reason other than commerce.

Inside, I pulled the jar of honey from the cupboard. It was only the second jar we had had in over a year. The jar felt warm, as though the amber was creating its own heat. There was no sound from Flannery or Isla, so I opened the jar with a soft click. The smell was powerful. Anything that didn't smell like salt or water was powerful. I dipped my little finger in, just the tip, and sucked the honey off. There was a shuddering of delight in my chest and I closed my eyes. The boat was shifting under my feet in its gentle undulation, and I breathed deeply, savouring the sweetness on my tongue.

The jar slipped from my hands and cracked against the floor. Shattered glass surrounded my bare feet in an instant, and the honey slipped easily through the cracked glass and onto the floor. I stared, disbelieving. With a crash, Flannery was at the bedroom door. His face paled as he saw the mess around my feet.

'I'm sorry,' I said. Isla appeared, rubbing her eyes. 'I'm sorry,' I said again. 'I was just tasting it.' The moment she realised what had happened, tears began sliding down her face.

'Don't move,' Flannery said. 'You'll hurt yourself.' I knew that, of course. I needed them to help. A simple cut, especially on a foot, could be fatal with our limited medical supplies. I didn't move, but neither did they. Moving would make my mistake real. Cleaning up the honey, the broken glass, would make it clear that neither of them would be able to taste that sweetness again for who knows how many months. Such a simple treat could become an emotional devastation in seconds. I closed my eyes, and waited for them to feel ready to help me. The sweetness on my tongue had turned grainy and sour.

* * *

I had a vague memory of beach holidays. My mother, my uncle, my sister and I, crammed into an old station wagon with a week's worth of food, clothes, games. Amber and I would be in the back, in charge of the snacks for the road. The power went to Amber's head once, and she refused to let me eat anything for the first two hours. Our furious, whispered fight – kept low because Mum was sleeping in the passenger seat – eventually grew too loud. When I yelped that Amber wasn't sharing the corn chips with me, my uncle said, 'Get them off her then,' and turned the radio up louder. The ensuing fight meant that the corn chips were spilled across the seat and crunched under her feet, we each came away with long pink scratches on our arms, and Amber had a choking fit that almost made her throw up. Mum woke up then, and Amber never refused to share the snacks with me again.

We had those holidays until I was thirteen, that's when the sea became too swollen to swim in, the roads too treacherous to drive, our land to precious to leave unattended. For thirteen years, the taste of salt water meant holidays, diving under waves, sunburn. It meant washing sand out of my swimmers at the end of the day, and finding grains in my hair for a week afterwards. It meant freedom and relaxation and ice-cream. Now, I barely noticed its constant burn in the back of my throat.

* * *

'Smoke,' Flannery said. He was standing at the window and Isla and I joined him. 'North east,' he said, but we already knew.

'Charlie's.' Isla and I looked at each other but none of us moved. We couldn't risk leaving our mooring, the posts that were high enough for us were rare, and we could see the boats chugging by, desperate to find somewhere to stop so they could use their petrol for a generator, not the engine. Someone called Flannery's name, and he went round the back to where our neighbour was calling.

'We should go,' Isla said.

'We can't.'

'But the goats…' The goats, we knew, would burn to death, and with them any chance of fresh meat in the next few months.

'Someone will get Charlie at least,' I said. She squeezed my hand, and we were both wondering if it was true, or if his charred corpse would float past us one day.

* * *

Charlie's corpse passed us two days later. It wasn't charred, he made it off his land, but the sea took him. He was bloated, his skin fragile from the salt water. Isla turned away, but Flannery and I stood and watched. Flannery hummed a song, but it was too faint for me to hear. It was the only memorial we could give him.

* * *

It was my day to visit Patricia, but when I arrived, I could tell from her face that it was a lost cause.

'Sorry, Pearl,' she said. 'They're just off their game at the moment.' She was leaning on the fence, watching the five chickens pick at the soggy ground. Her gumboots had mud crusted to the top.

I had only been ashore long enough to walk the three kilometres to her farm, and my legs were still unsteady on the solid ground. I held onto the fence next to her. She patted my arm.

'Come in for a cuppa, at least.'

Patricia lived in one room of a dilapidated house. The other rooms were falling into the sodden ground, but she had reinforced one. It used to be the porch, and she was able to add extra foundations before the ground gave way too much. Then all it needed was walls and a ceiling and it was sturdier than anywhere else for miles. We sat against the wall, our legs stretched in front of us, and watched the sea through the hole she uses as a door. Everything tasted like mud, but she didn't notice anymore.

The sea looked fat from here. On the boat, it was harder to tell. It could look silky even as it bloated towards the next storm. From here, it always looked too fat to exist, like there was some special gravity holding it back from rushing through the rest of the land. As though its meniscus had grown in strength as the water grew in volume, and it now simply stuck to itself where it would previously have rushed forward.

Of course, that was all in my head. It was my eyes playing tricks on me as they wished to see something other than the sea.

* * *

The first time the sea slipped over the tide barrier was a one-off, of course. A once-in-a-lifetime catastrophe that hungry townspeople recorded on their cameras as a record to show their grandkids one day. The mayor appeared on the local news talking about how well we had responded to the threat. The head of the emergency services looked like he had been drunk for days, his ruddy cheeks barely able to contain his grin as he talked about how proud he was of his team.

The following year they ran out of sandbags, because they had presumed the once-in-a-lifetime catastrophe wouldn't happen again so quickly. By the time I was twenty, the tide barrier was permanently under water.

* * *

'No eggs,' I said, squeezing my sweating feet out of my gumboots and leaving them to the side. The listing of the boat suited me, and I immediately felt steadier. Isla and Flannery had dripping rags in their hands and were doing the rounds of the hinges, the nuts and bolts, all the metal that threatened to give way under the weight of water. They stopped what they were doing.

'None at all?' Isla asked.

'It's okay,' Flannery said. He wiped the back of his hand across his forehead in a caricature of a tired man. I couldn't see it, but I knew he had just wiped grime across his skin and he would be feeling the individual particles gritting to him.

Was this an emergency? was the thought we were all having. Our emergency supplies had been eaten away at an increasing pace over the last six months. Emergency had become a normal state but some day, one day, we'd have to recalibrate what we meant by the word. Was today that day? I could see in Flannery's eyes that he was having the same thought. Isla was hungry. She was pre-menstrual, and we needed to take that into consideration. We always did. Some days, this day, she needed more than us. I suspected that I wouldn't need those extra rations for much longer, if ever again, but I was ten years older than her. All of this we had to factor into our choices.

CHRIS HANCOCK

A Hard Place to Love

Synopsis

2005. Fleeing the end of a toxic relationship, British drama student JOSH arrives in Russia vowing to focus on his dissertation, but he soon meets beguiling fellow actor, ALEKS. Aleks draws him into the murky queer sub-culture of St Petersburg where Josh encounters VADIM, a bitter old queen, who entices him with stories of the Blue Lab – a gay dissident group. Josh delves into the Soviet archives and discovers that Aleks' long-lost father (a leading member of the Blue Lab) was murdered whilst cruising for sex and his killer was never caught. When Aleks discovers the truth it sets him and Josh on a collision course with Aleks' mother, VERA.

Vera – a respected traffic cop – has spent a lifetime lying about her husband's death. When a political promotion triggers a spate of blackmail, accusing her of murder, she's adamant she is innocent, and calls on her loyal lover, ZHDANOV, to help unmask the perpetrator. Her investigation collides with Josh's digging in the KGB archives, but when she tracks him down to a gay nightclub, she is devastated to find Aleks there too.

Evidence of Vadim and Zhdanov's criminal past comes to light and Vera, Josh and Aleks form an uncomfortable alliance as they shun former loyalties in an attempt to find the truth. They use the drama school's gala performance to set an audacious trap where Vadim – obsessed with retribution – outs himself as the blackmailer. Guilt-ridden, Zhdanov reveals his key role as a KGB agent within the Blue Lab, covering up the murder to protect Vera. An autopsy report reveals that Vera's violent assault on her husband, just days before his death, led to an aneurism that ultimately killed him. Now, with the truth known, both couples (Josh and Aleks, Vera and Zhdanov) must decide if their relationships can survive.

* * *

Leningrad, USSR, 24th June 1986

The bathroom was the only safe place in a communal apartment. Vera locked herself inside and knelt down on the cool tiled floor. Sick with dread she unfolded the newspaper – *Leningradskaya Pravda*, the early morning edition. She soon found what she was looking for, there, on the inside page. A headline. Bold and undeniable.

Our public parks will be swept clean of such defilement!

Beneath the proclamation was a short column which she forced herself to read.

Yesterday evening a disturbance took place in Yusupov Gardens, near the palace steps. There occurred a confrontation between individuals of immoral lifestyle, which escalated, resulting in deadly violence. The victim, a young male, received multiple stab wounds to the upper back. He wore a distinctive yellow shirt and carried a guitar in a leather case. Any witnesses should contact Leningrad municipal police.

Vera felt briefly euphoric. The article made no mention of the victim's name. Nothing to tie her to him. But then relief again gave way to torment as she saw the bloodied yellow shirt, the man spitting dirt from his lips as he hauled himself from under the canopy of trees. She felt his panic as her own, choking and gasping for life. She imagined how the sun, still high in the evening sky, would have bathed the body in a powdery yellow haze, and she imagined the stillness of death.

Inside her the baby began to kick and squirm. A relentless, remorseless reminder that for her, for them both, this was only the beginning.

Chapter 1

Nineteen years later

Fuck you, Barty, typed Josh in a jealous frenzy. *I choose Russia. Where, quite sensibly, they executed the upper classes with a bullet to the back of the head.*

Josh had never been to Russia, but he'd studied the history, theatre, literature and he knew it to be a land of suffering. He also knew that to emerge finer and stronger, a person had to suffer. That to progress in this or any life you had to endure ordeal by fire. So be it, he decided. Russia was not the easy choice, but it was the truest one.

And it's a thousand miles away from you, you cheating little shit...

* * *

On the far side of the vast studio a girl with a pixie cut of pink hair was rummaging through one of the curtains. She moved anxiously from one window to the next, shaking out the folds of each tall black curtain. Having ruffled them all, she clasped her head and moaned. The rest of the students watched intently from their semi-circle. No one had noticed Josh's late arrival.

Flushed, the girl stepped towards the ring of chairs. 'Am I done?'

'How do you feel?' said the Master. He was short and bald with a thick black beard and, apart from the pink-haired girl, was the only one standing.

'Worked up,' she replied.

'And where is the money?'

She shifted her weight.

'You were looking for five thousand roubles,' said the Master. 'Did you find it?'

'There was no money,' she said, confused. 'I was pretending.'

With a smile, the Master removed his glasses and rubbed them on his tie.

'What I meant,' said the girl quickly, 'is that it didn't come naturally to me in this room, with all this light, without any props. Perhaps if I had a stage.'

'This room is your stage,' said the Master, 'and will be your stage for the next four years.'

Josh's stomach lurched. Four years seemed an incredible stretch. He reassured himself that his commitment to the institution was ten months tops. Until July. He would perfect his Russian, drink the theatrical elixir, and piss off back home.

'What we saw from you, Tonya, was amateurish and naïve. You had no intention of finding the money at all, instead, we all observed you *searching* for it. You wished to create an impression, and that cannot be called acting.'

Tonya was on the verge of tears as the Master dismissed her back to her seat.

'You're late,' he said. The attention of the room pivoted to Josh.

'The foreigner,' someone whispered.

Josh compelled himself forward, across the ancient parquet floor, and took the only empty chair. That morning's porridge, fried cheese toast, and four subsequent coffees were repeating on him.

'Where have you been?'

How could he admit that he almost hadn't come? How could he convey the loneliness of the six stifling weeks he'd already spent in a homestay with a batshit family, trying to improve his Russian? This very morning, he'd sat for hours in a coffee shop opposite the Lufthansa offices, daring himself to cross the road and buy a plane ticket home.

'I lost myself,' said Josh, tripping up over the verb.

'Let's hope you find yourself,' said the Master, who now called for another student. After the car crash they'd just seen, there were no volunteers. Except one. One who rose above the ignominy of being picked by calmly raising her hand.

'Darya,' said the Master. 'Let's hope you have a better temperament for the exercise.'

Darya pitched herself straight into the centre of the room, her little rah-rah skirt – a bold choice given the morning's drizzly September weather – displayed the length of her tanned legs. Josh watched all the boys watching her. Watched one boy in particular, the one with the proud collarbone, washed-out denim shorts, grey t-shirt. His deep tan, like Darya's, flung Josh's mind back to summer, his own dreadful summer, festering in the city. In coffee shops, he'd slogged his way through the novel Dr Zhivago and taken up smoking as an ersatz hobby, a justification for being in public alone. He grew used to, then fond of, smelling of cigarettes. He never once phoned his mum, who'd warned him strongly against travelling to a 'gangster state'.

The Master was now repeating the rules of the exercise – find the banknote that was pinned somewhere in the curtains – asking Darya to do so *truthfully*. Josh counted twelve curtains in all, or six pairs, as she set off for the far end of the room. Her search was more thorough than Tonya's had been, feeling inside the hem, using the radiator as a plinth to search the upper reaches and the eyelets. Just observing this mundane search was fascinating. A sense she was alone at work as she took forever to inspect every fold of every curtain. At the penultimate curtain, she reached behind it and screamed with delight, pretending to pluck out the banknote, holding it in a fist raised high. She skipped to the middle of the studio and performed a victory twirl.

'Where is the money?' asked the Master.

Darya pretended to fold the non-existent note and slip it inside her bra. 'For safekeeping,' she said, a little self-consciously.

Master Filshtinskii circled the students. 'Darya started well,' he said. 'Her search was systematic, painstaking. A slower pace than Tonya. Turning up nothing with each curtain, she became more and more frustrated.' Darya was smiling proudly. 'But where did she go off track?'

The group, impressed with what they'd seen, were not expecting this. But Josh had noticed something. A subtle turning point. Anyone who'd read Stanislavski ought to have known the answer and he silently formulated a response. The Master first picked on a big lad called Pavel who shook his head. 'Dunno.'

The Master nodded towards Josh.

Josh cleared his throat. 'When Darya found the banknote,' he said, 'her performance began to change.'

Darya shot him a look that was quick and sour, layered with surprise. Filshtinskii turned a question back to the group. 'What changed? Let's be specific.'

Josh scratched his chest and waited.

'I hope you're not expecting the foreigner do all the heavy lifting?' said the Master, his jaw tightening, as though the very integrity of the Russian actor were at stake. Finally, he gestured for Josh to speak.

'She began to pretend. Her gestures became … bigger, like she had an audience. It was clear to me that she knew she was being watched.'

'She became conscious of the eyes of the audience,' said Filshtinskii. 'With the discovery of the cash, the desire to demonstrate became irresistible.'

'I don't like people staring at me,' she said.

'I don't believe that for a second,' said the boy in the denim shorts and everybody laughed. Darya loomed over him. 'There's a difference, Aleks,' she said, 'between watching and staring. Think you could do it better?'

So, this was Aleks, the one with the tan, and the shorts, the blunt cut fringe and the dirty smile, goading her. His legs were crossed at the knee, a position which Josh instinctively copied.

Darya returned to her seat, nominating Aleks to go next. Master Filshtinskii announced there would be a small change to the exercise for its third iteration and from his pocket he pulled a red banknote, a real five thousand roubles. The class was in uproar, crying foul that Aleks got to play the game for real cash. The Master shouted for silence. He reminded them that it was not, and never had been, a game.

'Can I keep the money?' asked Aleks.

Josh calculated five thousand roubles was worth about a hundred quid.

'You must find it first.'

But the class weren't letting it go. A short lad with shaved head stood up from his seat, echoing the discontent. 'Why should Aleks get the first shot?'

Filshtinskii seemed to sense the mood. 'In the spirit of equity,' he said, 'Aleks may choose a partner in the game. A fair fight. I'll stick the money somewhere in secret, and we will watch their search. I'll even put a time limit of five minutes. Whoever finds the money in that time, can keep it. Otherwise, another pair get a chance to go.'

'I don't need a partner,' said Aleks.

'Choose a partner,' said the Master, 'or forfeit your place.'

Aleks cast his eyes around the group. There was nothing more cringeworthy, thought Josh, than the desperation on everybody's faces, like kids wanting to be picked for the team in PE. Josh tried to look like he didn't care either way. Aleks spun around. Deciding. Russian roulette.

'Him,' said Aleks, pointing.

'Joshua?'

'Yep.'

'Why him?'

Aleks shrugged, but he had to give an answer. 'Because I know he'll let me find the money first.'

Laughter travelled round the circle. What did Aleks mean? That Josh would be a pushover?

'A selfish sentiment,' said Filshtinskii to Aleks. 'But you are faithful to your nature. That's important in an actor.' He ordered Aleks and Josh to leave the room whilst the money was hidden.

In the empty corridor they stood in silence. Josh wondered how to play it. The presence of real money transformed the exercise, raised the stakes. He wanted to ingratiate himself, sure, but he refused to be walked all over. That's exactly what had happened with Barty, his ex.

'Your hair,' said Aleks suddenly, as though noticing him for the first time.

Josh touched the top of his head self-consciously. Had he forgotten his hair wax?

'It's red, like Prince Gary.'

Prince Gary was what Russians called Prince Harry. Same with Gary Potter.

'Prince Gary's got ginger hair,' corrected Josh. 'Mine's red-brown.'

Aleks seemed to find this clarification amusing. 'I like it,' he said. 'It's rare.'

Josh felt his cheeks flush. 'I'm from England,' he said, by way of explanation.

'England?' said Aleks, a flash of curiosity passing through his cloud-grey eyes. Then he said something that Josh didn't fully catch, something like, 'My father's in England,' or 'My father's from England.' The latter seemed unlikely. Everything about Aleks spoke of a sober, Slavic heritage. Tanned skin pulled taut over high, arresting cheekbones, like a propaganda poster for *A Young Builder Of Communism!* Not a bit British, thought Josh. Even his gaze – cool and distant – seemed calibrated to a land of vast, sublime panoramas.

'Does that mean you speak English?' asked Josh, in English.

Aleks frowned. Apparently not. No matter. Josh preferred it that way. Full Russian immersion.

'What are you doing here?' asked Aleks.

Josh haltingly explained his intentions, to learn acting, side by side with his Russian classmates.

'I see,' said Aleks, in a tone that made Josh feel both very brave and perfectly mad.

'Um, and I have a dissertation to write.'

Aleks cleared his throat. 'What I just said before, about the money, about the game…'

'You were joking,' said Josh.

'No,' said Aleks, sharply. 'You must let me find the money.'

Confused, Josh asked, 'You want me to pretend?'

'Yes, pretend, but don't overdo it,' said Aleks. 'You can look for the money, shake the curtains, dash about. But don't *find* the money. Let me be the one who finds it.'

Josh was worried now that his search would look forced or false, and, like the kooky Tonya, he'd be judged an amateur on his first day. His standing in the group might never recover.

Aleks clicked his fingers. 'You listening? We don't have much time. You understand when I speak Russian, right?'

'I understand,' said Josh, bristling. 'But the Master will recognise if I'm pretending. That's the whole point of the exercise.'

Aleks sighed. 'The point of the exercise is to act like you're *not* pretending. The point is to make an impression of realism.'

Now Josh really was confused, his brain fogging up. A common occurrence when conversing in this country – a wicked concoction of tough vocabulary and universal Russian obstinacy.

Aleks attempted a smile, revealing strong white teeth. 'I don't think you need the money.' This was true. Josh's travel grant and student loans would stretch a long way in Russia. 'But I want the money,' said Aleks. 'This course is very expensive. And we Russians are poor.' He said all this with utter sincerity.

Josh fought the temptation to do what he was told by a good-looking young man.

'Let me find the money,' repeated Aleks, slipping his hands into his pockets. 'I'll make it worth your while.'

A pulse ran up Josh's spine, like quick hands climbing a rope. Had the door not opened at that moment, he might have conceded. Tonya ushered them back into the room, their classmates all giddy for the impending spectacle. Josh stood facing Aleks. They even shook hands as the good-natured creases fell from around Aleks' eyes.

'Ready?' said the Master.

'Ready,' said Aleks.

Whatever Josh had imagined for this moment abandoned him, leaving only the skin-crawling sensation of self-exposure. Icky and pleasant, like sinking into a bathtub of custard.

'Ready?' asked the Master.

Josh nodded.

'Then begin.'

HIGHLY COMMENDED

MÓNICA IBARRA PARLE

The River is a Brown God

Synopsis

The River is a Brown God *is a literary novel set in 1834 East Texas, when Americans were the illegal aliens, flooding over the Sabine River into the Mexican Republic.*

Marina Anaya (23) lives with her highwayman father and ailing mother on an isolated island in the marshes. American settlers sweep in from the east to coopt land and clear it for cotton farming. Marina's father vows to oust these slave-holding intruders from his territory.

But Marina dreams of life in the bright towns of the US among the glamorous people she sees on the steamboats chugging up the Sabine River. Enter Freddy Nash, a handsome man Marina meets near the island, and Marina can't stop thinking about him over the weeks that follow.

Only Freddy's not all that he seems: He's captivated by Marina, but he's also a product of his harsh world, and he's come to Louisiana to make his own fortune. He joins the army investigating piracy in the bay and potential victims of Father's.

As Mamá's condition worsens, Father becomes more desperate, and becoming increasingly suspicious of Marina, who's sneaking off to meet Freddy. In a fit of fury, he disowns Marina, and she flees to Freddy.

The more Marina glimpses Freddy's world, the more she comes to see that it's not at all what she'd dreamed of: it's a fraught place full of inherited colonial divisions, and she encounters first-hand the slave smuggling that fuels border commerce. Marina begins to suspect that Father is the only man courageous enough to stand against the spoiling settlers.

When the fight comes, Marina must be ready to keep the land and the legacy she holds dear, even when everyone she loves is lost, and she must find a way to begin again.

1

Tejas, the First Mexican Republic, 1834

Gators roam my father's waters. Bass and catfish too. Snakes that twitch their rattle tails, moccasins, and copper-mouths. Pines and bald cypress grow thick and close, creeping furry roots into Father's streams. Black bears, bobcats, and razorbacks hunt among their trunks. The marshes are morasses of sucking mud and constrictor vines, and poisoned ivies we have no callus for. A horse-plough left a pair of hours will vanish in the brush. But Father's waters put a hex round us, making a veil between our world and the next. For a long while, we're happy and alone in our wet world.

Until the Norteños get wind of our fertile soil and long growing season – perfect cotton country, their newspapers say. Promise in Tejas – theirs for the taking. They can do what the Spanish could not, making these lands the richest this world – new or old – has yet seen. There are rivers ready to shuttle cotton down to the bay, across to New Orleans, and from there, the old world. Norteño settlers locked out of the Gulf states start spilling over the river, fencing off fields and forcing the waters' course. They bring their slaves in chains and cinch the mighty trees tight around their trunks, strangling them to clear our forests field by field.

All the while, Father and his waters wait to strike. Clouds crowd; gray sheets you see for hectares, then the heavens rend and Father's waters spurn their banks. They dash and swallow, sucking mud and seeds to their depths, swilling it around. Father and his waters take their treasures and transform them, lay them back upon the shores fresh and new and free. When the waters recede, the trees fruit with leather boots and ploughs and corpses, hanging in their boughs a garish lace.

For a while, this ensures the colonists don't stay. Their hopes dashed in the river's fury, they straggle west for more solid ground. For a while, it keeps them away.

But a time does come.

* * *

I first see the stranger by the mission graveyard. It's a spit of land, bound by Father's waters on all sides but one. The sleepers here are foreign dead. Not Father's. He buries at sea or in hides you won't find. To my knowing, he's never ventured here. Still as everywhere on the eastern fringes of the Republic – his waters snake the edge of the plot, making the soil so black and fertile that hyacinth and hummingbird vines creep from old bones.

As I pick a wild posy, the bass surface, pipping gummed lips over the water. A harsh sound: like men drowning, bubbles rising and bursting on the surface, but lulling too if you know the cause. Flick flick flick. A sign of aloneness, though not loneliness. Precious life in a back-water. I pause to listen, then comes the slap of oars. A boat, pushing through the rushes. Too early for Father. I throw myself flat upon my belly and pray the alien vessel will hurtle on by.

Instead a buckskin-smooth voice rises up – a man, singing in English, a song so sweet, I've never heard the like. A young couple, he croons, and a morning, and a fertile valley. What gossamer, I think, as by and by, a craft scuttles into view. It bears no semblance to Father's. Small and wooden, but not hewed from a single cypress like ours are. Foreign wood cut into short planes fixed neat together. Fresh stained – with care too. Not the slapdash of Father's love.

In the boat, a man traveling alone. For all his wild ways, Father *always* surrounds himself with men. Creole trappers, the ne'er-do-well braves he's lured from one tribe or another, the coyote bloods, and runaway men. Father's never once missed his shadow. Perhaps because he knows better than most how easily a body can vanish in these marshes.

The cloud sits low, turning the light odd and the water so silvery, even the craggy trees look like good witches. Still, this ain't no fertile, love-lorn valley. Strangers keep well away from here, having heard rumors of banditry and thieves.

But no. His song turns to a hanging, and even I could not have imagined our fertile valley would lead us here, though that is much closer to the life I know. He's just a ordinary man then, hands and heart and fears – all human.

"And me neck will pay for all," he sings. "When I die, when I die."

He may soon get his wish, if he carries on so. He sings so loud and clear, he's either stupidity personified or the boldest dog that ever lived. To paddle sure and happy and *so loudly* into these lands. What a fool. Or perhaps he's up to some foul trick.

I check I have the hooked blade in my boot. I ruck my skirts for better purchase and watch, fingers clutching the bone hilt as the stranger oars forward.

He's pale like Father, and me, but unlike us, this stranger's not a whisker dark. To look upon his face, I feel those bass-bubbles flicking over my skin. Red-gold hair hits his collar, and a rasp of ginger across his chin and cheeks. A Norteño, then. No doubt making his way from that young nation that stretches far beyond the Sabine. He wears a simple suit and a battered hat, the brim tipped back to little shade his face. The effort of paddling has made his cheeks bright as the wine cups that grow behind our lodge. His boat's piled with provisions and a carpet bag says he means to stay a while.

I shift to track him. My scrabbling sends the grackles keening up. The stranger's gaze darts toward the grasses that shield me. His face alights, and his laugh's a ringing thing like water pinging a tin pail.

"You gave me fright." He clutches his chest and laughs some more.

The stranger's mirth's foreign as his boat and those songs of his. I remain half-crouched, fingers tightening on my knife. I'd have been better prepared had he come with pistols drawn. That's a pose I understand. But not this – not laughter and songs. What can he possibly want here? Still I refuse to let him think I'm a one to take a challenge lying down. That's not how Father raised me. I take my blade's hilt, hide it in my skirt, and press up to stand.

He doffs his hat. "You speak English?"

I nod, but will not give him a one wit more. My English is good enough, French too, and even Caddo, Hasinai, and Comanche. I speak them near as well as Spanish, for we're a mish-mash of peoples here. These lands so far from the central valley, the ousted Crown once took any wretch willing to farm a plot of land to hold this precious territory in their coffers. On this account, the Crown blundered badly, opening their borders to the Norteños in the first place.

The stranger ponders his hat, cheeks pinking all the more, as if he'll find his next words stitched into the grimy band. "Forgive me, miss. I didn't expect to see a soul. I wouldn't dream of plaguing a lady with such a song. My god, what must you think of me?"

I want to blurt, why I think nothing at all of you, or so Father would surely want me to say. Only the stranger looks so shamefaced, but there's a lightness too. A laugh held just in check. All that feeling jimmied into one handsome face.

"You think I'm some fragile thing?" I want to spur that mirth on. "I stand knee deep among the dead." I wave at the rotting crosses.

He casts a wry look at the graves. "Perhaps it's to them then that I should atone. To taunt them so," he says, clicking his tongue at his cheek. "What shame I bring, but I spose they cannot truly fault me. Not seeing as they have no hearts or souls, not underground at least. And it's the fools truth, had I known a girl such as you were here I'd never have thought to woo you with such a song."

"Pshaw. Now that's the far more foolish tack to take," I say.

He scrunches the hat and then seeing what he's done, tosses it on the bench behind him. He takes a moment to tame the wild curls he's unleashed.

It's a pleasant voice you have, I want to add, but bite my tongue so hard I taste rust. What fool I am too, for this ain't no place for idle paddles. He has come here a purpose, and Father would never forgive me if I gave him reason to stay a moment longer. I must usher him along, for his sake and mine.

"Sir, I do not know you," I say, "but I do know that you'd best not be on my father's land."

He mimes confusion. "This is a graveyard, is it not?" He makes a show of the rotting crosses. "Your father's a ghost? Will he rise to smite me like a vampyre?" He curls his fingers, mocking bear perhaps, not devil. There's a lilt to his voice, an accent that speaks of lands across seas.

I laugh though again, I know better. It seems what I know has departed my every sense now this stranger has come. Vampyre or ghost Father's not, but if only this stranger knew how close he's come. I straighten to look formidable in spite of dirty skirts.

"My father does not take kind to strangers."

My tone's fierce as any of Father's men, but it's hard to hold fearsome when standing with skirts rucked over muddy knees. The tall grass may shroud all sacred flesh, but I can feel something akin to those bass bubbles on my skin as his eyes drift down. He lingers a moment too long. Then his eyes dart up, cheeks ruddier – flushed now a hue so scarlet I'm near afeared for his life. Never mind Father. His eyes skate to the bare skin of wrists poking out of my cuffs.

"The man – " he stammers, and I am gratified to see he too is misfooted.

"The man?" I prod.

He closes his eyes, as if to collect his thoughts. "The man I spoke to in Lafitte said these lands are untitled. Told me they're free to any who would take them."

A hawk screeches downriver, and I check again to make certain it's not been disturbed by someone else paddling there.

"They are not – untitled, I mean. All this belongs to my father." I pause. "And last I heard, no more Norteño settlers should cross that river."

"I mean no harm." He raises his hands before his chest, palms out. "Trouble is, Miss, I find myself off course. I had no intention of crossing. I'm new to Louisiana. Made my way south from Pennsylvania – "

"But your accent – "

He seems pleased I've noticed. "I came as a boy. From Derbyshire – that's in England."

I cut him off. "We got maps here, too. Even in a backwater. And judging by your blunder here, our maps are better than yours."

That laugh again. "I came on a contract. Just worked myself free after fourteen years."

I've heard of the Norteños' labor contracts – poor children brought in ships and starved and worked into the ground until they've paid off a debt. Theirs, their parents', or whoever had leave to sell their labor. The stranger and I watch each other a minute. There they go again, bass-bubbles, popping along my skin. Not entirely unpleasant, but like the sound, it's good and also akin to drowning.

"Now you're off course?" I prompt.

"I paddled out, you see, to get a sense of the land, and the river forked. It's only now you speak I wist I took the wrong route." He gestures helplessly back.

His eyes are changeable as agate: slate and river-water blue and the same green of the trees on water. Finally they flick away as that hawk calls her alarm again down river. I tilt my head, listening for any sound upon the water. The stranger wouldn't be grinning so if he knew this is the very last turn he should've took. For even now Father and his men will be taking up their arms and pushing their boats onto the water.

I must send him on. Without delay.

"Closest town is Lafitte, which I'd reckon is the way you've come."

"Could you show me?" He pauses. "I'd happily escort you back after. And then you could escort me, and I you. Back and forth. We could make a game of it – " That grin again.

I shake my head. "Couldn't even if I wanted to. We got no truck with towns."

The stranger ponders me a minute. A mosquito whirrs at his chin, and he scratches, leaving raised welts. More come and cluster at his neck and wrists. He swats these too away. They won't stop coming now the welts offer blood. It all comes down to weakness round here.

"What's your name?" Agate eyes search my face.

"Marina."

Now, why in heavens have I gone and done that? Most times, that word's a figment on my tongue. A me I keep locked up tight in a trunk. It's been so long since anyone used it, in fact, that I often worry I'll forget. It's just that names are everything to Father. Fit only for those who know you best, those who will care and treasure them. Father believes your name's a magic spell that binds you till your death. Strangers will only use them to lock you in a cell. Father wakes screaming most nights, and he holds to his breast everything about himself from before he came to this place. The man he once was is a mystery. And so far as I can tell, his name's got much to do with it, for he keeps it more precious than all the gold in his store-house. And Mamá only calls me *querida.* It'd be a fool thing if I wanted this stranger to know me true. But even if I wanted, I now can't pluck those siren-sounds from the air between us.

"Marina."

I watch it on his lips.

Bass bubbles dance along my flesh. He says it again, so softly – a treasured thing. A little voice inside says to ask his name, but I tamp it down. Why in god's name do I care? I'll never see him again. It'd be a fool thing for him to hang around here. There is no future between us. No way two souls from the wrong sides of the river could find a way to belong.

SUSAN KEMP

Wildish

Synopsis

This wildlife crime detective story centres a former army intelligence officer, Jessie MacInally, as she transfers her skills from uncovering poaching networks in Africa to working as an investigator for a newly established forensics laboratory specializing in wildlife crime in Scotland.

The story opens with the theft of pair of golden eagle's egg and the killing of the female bird. This happens shortly before Jessie arrives at Heughie Glen in the dark of an autumn evening to visit her dad, Dewar, a gamekeeper struggling to manage in impoverished conditions and with a new employer who wants rid of him. He has been accused of killing the eagle, something Jessie knows he would never have done. Newly contracted by the forensics lab, in partnership with Police Scotland's Wildlife Crime Unit, to source evidence leading to convictions with custodial sentences rather than just fines, Jessie takes this as her first case.

Separately, environmental scientist Gregor Phelan has asked the lab for help in exposing a leak within the impact reporting system. A recent discovery of a thriving freshwater pearl mussel habitat would have prevented the building of a new wind-farm except, coincidentally, the habitat was destroyed shortly after the report was submitted. The lab enlists Jessie into Gregor's plan and she sets herself up as a walker and wildlife photographer for cover.

First, Jessie follows the birder who killed the eagle and finds enough evidence to also arrest him for the eagle killing. While she is doing that, Phelan submits a fake environmental impact report, which establishes a new freshwater habitat in Glen Heughie, and they set up a watch. It's not long before their plans unravel as the gang sent to destroy the habitat discovers they are being watched and decides to exact revenge.

Chapter One

It's still light as he arrives home. He parks his car in the drive and, after plugging it into charge, stands for a moment in the early evening quiet, soaking up the change in season. Spring is upon them and the air feels different, almost excitable. Sounds leaking through open windows travel through the evening with a crispness he doesn't remember hearing over winter.

He allows himself another moment of anticipation about the coming week before turning and entering the house. He fights the instinct to lower his head, forgetting the low ceilings and the tiny rooms until their physical presence reminds him. Before Chloé, he and Liz had lived in the upstairs flat of a converted Edwardian house. They had fallen in love with its one huge room with high, corniced ceilings — never mind the box-like kitchen with the toilet off, and that badly installed shower. They only really noticed a problem when Liz fell pregnant and they'd tried to visualise where the baby would fit.

That baby hadn't lived, but by then they'd already installed themselves into this affordable and unbearably cheerful new-build house in the suburbs of Edinburgh's ever-growing developments. After giving birth to a dead baby Liz had found a sense of security and ease in their small cage, watched over by neighbours who never left her alone for long enough to wallow in grief. She'd wanted to stay even after they realised that the three beds, bath & liv/kitch house, as advertised, had somehow been magically squeezed into less overall space than the flat. And eventually, two years later and after 9 months of high anxiety and bed rest, Chloé had arrived by caesarian section on warm summer evening.

He hangs up his coat and steps into the living room where Liz and Chloé are curled up on the sofa watching Eastenders and sipping tea.

'Hey,' he says.

'Hey Dad,' Chloé answers.

Liz looks up from the TV, 'How was work?'

'You know.

'Did Mrs F insist on…'

'Shhh…I'm watching.' Twelve-year old Chloé hates to chat.

He smiles and pushes himself between his daughter and her mother, stealing Chloé's mug of tea from her unsuspecting hands as he nudges her off the sofa.

'Oi…'

'You're lucky I don't make you fetch my slippers.'

'Hah, that's not fair. Give me my tea back.'

'Awww, won't you make your tired, old, hard-working faither a cup of tea?'

'Daaahad. I'm missing the best bit.'

He hands Chloé back her tea and sneaks a quick kiss on her forehead, 'All right, my sweet. I'll leave you be.'

He gets up from the sofa and walks three steps to the kitchen area to put the kettle on. Liz follows.

'What's for supper?' he asks.

'We're going to Jim and Hilda's.'

'We're not? Tell me you're winding me up?'

'I'm not and we are.'

'Shit. But I've got to pack.'

'You've been packing all week.'

'They'll make us play charades.'

'Consider it time served. I washed your camping towel and your walking socks. They're hanging up in the garage. I was thinking that maybe next year you could take Chloé with you?'

He is glad he has his back to his wife so she can't see his expression. Taking Chloé would mean the end of it all. He doesn't think he can do that.

Liz continues talking as she gets the milk out of the fridge and passes it to him, 'She was talking about your week and seemed to think it sounded fun. I reminded her, of course, of how much she hates going for walks with us on weekends but she claims that's different. I tried to explain that it's a hideous rain-filled torture where you have to dig holes for your own poo, but she told me I'm a wuss.'

He pauses then answers brightly, 'She'll be thirteen next year. I bet you a million pounds that by then she'll be pretending, as soon as we leave the house, that she's never even so much as met me before.'

'Oh my God,' Liz feigns terror, 'you're so right.' She looks over to her daughter for a moment. 'Oh how I look forward to those older teenage years.'

After an early start the next morning, he drives north for two hours before arriving at the foot of the Glen. He drives all the way up to the reservoir and beyond until he reaches a small cluster of trees near the end of the road. He takes out his rucksack with lightweight tent attached and hides it between a couple of tree trunks well back from the road. He checks that it can't be easily spotted from any angle, then gets back into the car and drives away. It's important that no one sees his car waiting for him at the foot of the hills. It would act like a big neon sign pointing right at him. Instead, he takes the car all the way back to Forfar where he parks it in the Co-op carpark. He walks the fifteen miles back to the reservoir at a pace. Night is well and truly fallen by the time he starts up the hill but the moon is big and bright and lights his way along the cat tracks. He makes good progress and decides to set up camp around 9.30pm.

His tent takes 5 mins and 40 seconds to erect. It is a piece of design brilliance that keeps him warm and dry even in the harsh storms which wash the hills of Perthshire with abundance. He re-fills his water container from the river and starts boiling some rice, dried mushrooms and onion on the camping stove. When it's ready he cuts some salami and sits cross-legged on the mossy banks of the river and chews thoughtfully.

In the moonlight, the heather and moss take on a strange silvery glow. It's so still that he can hear for miles: the scratching of a small animal – a fox? The scrunch of human footsteps on gravel – a sheep moving up the stony track behind him? He never gets the heebie-jeebies anymore, but nor does he forgot how easy it is to turn the night sounds into terrifying harbingers of doom. Sometimes he misses the added adrenaline rush but those small bursts made for equally small lows and those make you stupid. He can't afford to be stupid.

He takes his dishes down to the river and washes them with eco-soap. He uses the same soap to wash his face and hands. Back at the tent and with everything squared away, he pours himself a gill of whisky, his ration for the night, from a repurposed plastic water bottle and spreads his map out on the ground in front of him. The light from his head torch can be seen for miles so he uses it only in emergencies. Instead, he places a little cigarette torch about a centimetre above the surface of the paper and allows a small spill to illuminate the lines and codes that will guide him tomorrow.

Later, as he sleeps, the wind picks up and slaps the material of his tent with furious energy. Once woken, the noise keeps him awake. He pops his head outside and the racket is miraculously transformed into the gentle movement and sway of a strong breeze through long grass and hard heather. Since there isn't a sniff of rain he drags his sleeping bag and air-filled mat outside and sleeps en plein air instead. With his head wrapped in an all-weather head gaiter underneath a woollen hat he feels as protected from the cold as he would have been inside the tent. He loves the sense of the wind, and the feel of space. He feels like a better man.

He puts everything at risk for this experience. It is enough to remind him why he lives the life he does – why he should value the safety and security of a decent salary, even if the job is as boring as any job could possibly be, and hot water on tap. It might make a nonsensical explanation if he is ever caught, but he believes it. He knows he might be mentally dead without this.

The next morning he rises before dawn and packs up in a few minutes. He walks with his binoculars at the ready and stops to study the horizon every few minutes. The hills are not high but once he's left the cat tracks the terrain is rough going: a mix of boggy peat and high heather. Each step, he calculates, takes at least ten percent more effort than on a track.

Over the course of the next three days he sees one of either of the two golden eagle three times before he finds them both on the fourth. They soar across the skyline with magnificent grace: their wingspan and ruthless talons from a different time. They don't seem to fit this era of redbrick cul-de-sacs and breathable Gortex. He sees one bird swoop behind a forest of pine and emerge with a swinging carcass. Probably a hare. It's a wondrous sight, almost impossible to believe. It feels like something you'd see in Game of Thrones not something so viscerally real. He watches where the eagle goes and follows.

He spots the eyrie from a mile away. It's on a ledge high on a cliff between the slopes of two of the steeper hills. He circles the upper slopes until he finds a route down from the top. Once there he has a clear view into the nest and knows he's timed it perfectly. There are two eggs and the female nowhere to be seen. That means the eggs are at least two weeks old, or thereabouts. The female would roost for that long before leaving the nest, now and then, to join in the hunt but only for very short periods and, often, the male would take over incubation. He'd have a very short window of opportunity.

He takes up a position far enough away so that his presence won't disturb the birds but where he can still get a good view, not only of the eyrie but of its surroundings too. He hides his rucksack in a deep patch of unruly heather and settles in to wait. He stays there for the rest of the day, watching and waiting. He eats salami and oatcakes and drinks the rest of the water. He doesn't bother unpacking his tent or his stove. When night comes, he lays in the heather fully clothed and wraps his unzipped sleeping bag around him. He resists the temptation to look again and repeatedly down at the eyrie. He doesn't want to spook the birds.

At dawn he is primed and ready. As soon as the birds leave to hunt, and as quietly as is possible, he sets up his ropes and abseils down the cliff-face to the nest. He scans the horizon constantly but sees nothing to worry about. It's easy. He takes one of the eggs and wraps it in bubble wrap, places it in a box and then into his daypack before climbing back up the cliff-face. He won't take both. Some would but not him. He is pleased with himself for resisting the temptation.

He hears it before he sees it. The sound of the flap of air beneath a large wing. He looks around just as the female lowers her legs and points her talons in the direction of the egg thief. They are massive and muscular and they descend like wheels from a landing aircraft. He takes the BB gun from his breast pocket and fires once. The eagle squawks and flaps and falls out of the sky like a stone. But just before she hits the ground she recovers and climbs unsteadily back towards him. He shoots it again and this time she lands with a thunk. Broken and dead. Massive. Her beautiful wings buckled beneath her weight.

He finishes his climb to the surface quickly, finds his rucksack and repacks it with his new trophy carefully placed between the towel and spare clothes. He descends the hill and walks toward the dead bird. He pauses to lean over the corpse and pull three feathers from the tail. He puts them in his pocket before marching out of the wilderness at a military pace.

When he returns to the cul-de-sac he places this newest trophy in amongst the collection at the back of the garage. The collection of over forty bird eggs stored inconspicuously in old margarine tubs. A collection his wife believes hasn't grown since her grandfather-in-law's death over four decades ago.

ZOE McCANN

Emails from Keats

Synopsis

Self-confessed bookworm Aoife Lockhart isn't remotely scarred by her dad's suicide. If anyone's scarred, it's her mum, Pauline, who channels her fury over Owen Lockhart's decision to jump out in front of a train into a macabre stand-up routine. If that's not a clear example of someone repressing their grief, Aoife doesn't know what is.

Anyway, Aoife's far too busy trying to work out who's been sending her the emails she's been getting from someone claiming to be the poet John Keats to dwell on her dad's death. Whoever it is, they seem to know all about her PhD on Keats's poetry, which makes her think it has to be one of four people: her friend Jude; her PhD supervisor, Dominic; or one of the students she shares an office with – the relentlessly negative Brendan or the androgynous, cape-wearing Fabian.

But when her paper is accepted for a conference in Edinburgh and she decides to stay with Elspeth, her dad's aunt, in his hometown of Lenzie, Aoife is finally forced to confront the question of why Owen killed himself. With Fabian and her mum in tow, she starts to unearth facts about her dad's life that make her question everything she thought she knew about him. After learning he witnessed his mother, Agnes, kill herself in the same way he did, she starts to suspect his own suicide is linked to his childhood trauma. And when a body recovered from a local nature reserve is identified as Owen's father, Douglas, she realises all the evidence points to Agnes having killed him.

As Aoife and Fabian work together to solve the mystery of what happened to Owen, they grow closer and Aoife starts to process her grief. The novel ends with Aoife deciding it was her dad who wrote the emails and scheduled them to be sent to her following his suicide. However, in the Epilogue, the reader learns it is Elspeth who is behind the emails.

PROLOGUE
OWEN
New Year's Day 2019

He's taking extra special care this morning. He had the nightmare again last night, and he can't seem to shake the uneasy feeling it's left him with. It was probably the prosecco that did it – full of sugar, that stuff, he doesn't know how Pauline can drink it – but still. It can't hurt to be thorough. He puts his shoes on, then his coat. Does up the studs from top to bottom, then checks for wallet and keys. Hat on. Another check. Right foot in the centre of the mat. Two clicks of his teeth on the left side, two clicks on the right. If he can get to the end of the sequence, everything will be fine. As long as no one interr–

"Dad."

He looks up to see Aoife standing at the bottom of the stairs in her pyjamas, holding a glass of water.

"Mm?"

"Mum says lunch is at one."

"Okie doke. Sore head this morning?"

"I'm a mere husk," she mumbles, rubbing her eyes. "If you have poison for me, I will drink it."

He laughs. "Shakespeare, is it?"

"It's always Shakespeare."

"Except when it's Keats."

"I don't deserve to quote Keats today," she says mournfully, trudging back up the stairs. "I'm away to die."

He chuckles. "See you later."

Where was he? Start again. Step back off the mat. Check for wallet and keys. Right foot on mat, get to the door. Clicking of teeth. Everything is fine.

"I'm off!" he shouts to Pauline, then pulls the front door behind him and sets off down the road. Where will he go today, he wonders? Dickensian London, maybe. They watched an adaptation of *A Christmas Carol* last week and it's been rumbling around in his head ever since. Pauline's always asking him how come he never gets bored of this same circuit – down to the King's Hall, along Balmoral Avenue, up the Malone Road and back down Finaghy Road South – but what she doesn't realise is that it's never the same to him because he's away in a different world each time. Yesterday he was selected to go and start the first human colony on Mars and he was making a video diary for the documentary. He'd be embarrassed to tell Pauline that, in case she thought he was silly. Pauline is very much a real-world sort of person. Aoife would understand, he thinks, but they don't talk about those sorts of things.

He feels better today, more like himself. He hasn't had the dream since Christmas morning. Writing it down seemed to get rid of it somehow.

He's just started to furnish the room in his modest Victorian bedsit when his mobile goes off. Elspeth, it has to be. Or Pauline, to tell him to get something. No one else phones him. He pulls his phone out of his pocket. Sure enough, it's Elspeth. Strange, though, given that he spoke to her on Christmas Day. Normally they'd leave it now until the next big occasion. He feels a mild stab of fear as he answers.

"Hi Elspeth. Happy New Year."

"Same to you, love. Where are you?"

"I'm just out for a walk. Is everything okay?"

"Oh, everything's grand. There's been a bit of funny news here this morning, though. They found a body in the Moss."

"Did they?"

"Aye. Pulled it out of the bog. A man, they say. They don't know how long he was there."

Something strange is happening to Owen. His heart has begun to hammer in his chest, and he feels cold all over.

"A man?"

"Aye. These peat bogs, you know, there's something in them that preserves a body. He could've been in there for years. I suppose they'll be doing tests and the like. But people are saying now we've got a murderer on the loose in Lenzie, and Moira next door's telling me I shouldn't be living on my own and I need one of these alarms and I don't know what to make of it all. I don't want anyone trying to put me in a home, Owen. I've lived in this house for 57 years and the only way I'm leaving it is in a box."

Owen's throat is closing over. "No one's going to make you go anywhere. You can come and stay with us if you're scared."

"Oh, I'm not scared," Elspeth says quickly. "Just a bit shaken up, is all. Oh no, I'm not scared. I just thought it was strange."

"It is, aye."

"It could turn out to be some Neanderthal man. I think Moira just likes any excuse to meddle in my business."

"I'd say you're right. Listen, Elspeth, I need to go here, I'm at the shop."

"You go, dear. I'll keep you posted."

"Thanks. You take care."

There's a thought trying to push its way into his consciousness, but he can't access it. It's got something to do with the nightmares he's been having. Another walker passes him and gives him a strange look. Two black spots appear in front of his eyes. They've found a body in the Moss. Someone has their arms around him, holding him back.

He's at the turn-off to Balmoral station now. He makes it onto the empty platform and sinks to his hunkers, holding his hands to his head. He tries to breathe. A body in the Moss. He could've been in there for years. He grapples for the thought, but it keeps slipping from his grasp.

A train horn blasts in the distance. He looks up at the tracks.

He sees a wasteland of brown grass, and he hears Aoife saying *the sedge is withered from the lake, / And no birds sing.*

And all of a sudden, he remembers.

1
AOIFE
April 2019

Normally when I find myself in a situation I don't know how to handle, I ask myself: what would Keats do? Sometimes, like when I'm struggling to write a chapter of my thesis or trying to justify buying a new pair of shoes, this helps me see exactly what I should do (abandon the work and put the shoes on my credit card, obviously). Other times, it's less helpful. Like now, for instance. Because he might have packed an impressive number of trials into his short life, but I'm guessing Keats never found himself on a date with a poultry farmer.

"I collect guns," Trevor the farmer has just announced, like this is a perfectly normal hobby.

I try not to let the horror show on my face. "Guns," I repeat.

"Yeah."

"And do you…" I hesitate, wondering what the appropriate follow-up question to this is. "… Shoot things with them?"

He looks at me like I'm an idiot. "Yeah, of course. Birds and things."

"Birds," I echo. "Right." I take a sip of my drink to disguise my grimace. I'd been so worried beforehand about him noticing my thinning hair that it never even occurred to me he might turn out to be a horrible person. But the more he talks, the more I'm starting to think I should never have shouted down my intuitive distrust of anyone who claims to have graduated from the School of Hard Knocks. My eyes dart to the door. Can I just leave, I wonder? Would Keats leave? Or would he accept this waste of a perfectly good afternoon as part of the complex tapestry of pleasure and pain that constitutes our earthly existence?

A leer spreads across Trevor's face. "One time, right, there was this badger in my barn and I –"

"Sorry," I cut in abruptly, gesturing at the napkin I'm holding to my nose. "I might just go and…" I nod in the direction of the toilets.

"Has it stopped?"

"I think so," I say, gingerly pulling the napkin away. My nose started to bleed almost as soon as I walked into the bar. I assumed the strange look he gave me when we shook hands was because he'd clocked my receding hairline, but when he gestured at his own face and went "I think your nose might be…" I realised that my body had actually decided to sabotage my appearance in a whole other way.

"I'll grab us another drink," he says, despite the fact that I've barely touched mine. I watch him hop off his stool and trot up to the bar in his platform shoes. He definitely lied about his height, and I'm starting to think he might have lied about his age, too, because his own hairline looks suspiciously sparse for a twenty-eight-year-old's. I make a beeline for the toilets, fishing my phone out of my bag as I go. Bad dates might not be Keats's department, but they're definitely Jude's. She answers as I'm standing in front of the mirror, dabbing at the dried blood on my nose with a wet tissue.

"Oh no," she groans. "What's happened?"

"It's a disaster. We have nothing in common, Jude. He's nothing like his –"

"Is he married?"

I suppress a sigh. Jude's husband had an affair and now she's of the opinion that all men are philandering toads.

"No, he's not married. He shoots birds for fun and he's about six inches shorter than me. Do you remember Fathead Phil?"

"Oh God, don't tell me he's –"

"Worse," I interrupt. "Nastier."

"Where are you now?" she asks. "Did you get rid of him?"

"I'm in the toilets," I say, peering out of the narrow glass panel in the door to see where he is. "He's at the bar getting another round. I'm trapped."

"Go back out there and tell him you're not interested."

"I can't do that! God, this is a nightmare. I don't know what I was thinking."

"Didn't I tell you not to go north of Glengormley?"

"That would have left me with a ten-mile –" I clench my teeth. This is not the time to challenge Jude's dating rules. "Look, can you just tell me how to get out of here, please?"

"Is there a window?"

"Jude, I am not going out through the window," I say, even as I eye the tiny pane of frosted glass on the opposite wall. "That is so rude."

"Just tell him you voted Remain. No! Wait! Tell him you're a vegan."

"That's what you'd do, is it?"

"I wouldn't be there in the first place." She mutters something inaudible as if she's talking to someone else, which tells me she's still in the postgraduate centre with Brendan. After a moment, she's back. "Right, we're coming to get you."

"Jude, you can't make it obvious!"

She tuts. "Give me some credit. We'll be there in five."

"Don't bring Bren –" I start to say, but she's already hung up. Shit, I think. Brendan is the world's least tactful person, and I just know he'll be rubbing his hands with glee at the chance to watch this car crash unfold. I sigh and take one last look at my face in the mirror. I've managed to dislodge my foundation in my attempt to clean the blood off, so I now have a big red nose on top of everything else. I comb my hair forward with my fingers to try to cover up how thin it is at the front, and then I walk back out into the bar.

Trevor is already halfway down his second pint. He nods at my two full glasses of wine. "Seven quid a pop," he says gruffly. "Get them down you."

I resist the urge to point out that I didn't ask for another drink. Instead, I take a sip from one of the glasses and glance furtively at the door, wondering how fast Jude and Brendan can possibly get here.

"So have you been on many Tinder dates?" he asks.

"Not really," I lie, doing a mental inventory of all the terrible dates I've been on in recent months. An image of Hugh the Hoover looming at me, tongue poking out like a spear, flashes into my mind and I quickly push it away. "Have you?"

He chuckles darkly. "I've had a few melters, aye. This one doll wouldn't get into my tractor. I said to her, catch yourself on. You're lucky I'm even giving you a lift."

I'm beginning to think I got off lightly, being trapped in a bar with him. He tried to get me to commit to a hill walk, but I had the good sense to insist on meeting him in the Queen's quarter, recalling the solemn vow I made after llama trekking with Wonky-Eye Derek never to go on another date that involved me wearing wellies or being spat on. I have my own rules, even if they're not quite as stringent as Jude's.

He takes a swig of his pint and looks me up and down as though I'm livestock he's appraising. Is he going to ask me about my hair, I wonder? It's ramped up the shedding in recent weeks, to the point where I'm sure it must be noticeably thin now. I try to stop myself from touching it.

"So what is it you study again? English, is it?"

"Yeah."

"Good luck finding a job with that. Hoping to teach, are you?"

"Lecture, actually," I say. "I'm doing a PhD on Keats's poetry, and –"

"Bet that set your mum and dad back a penny or two," he smirks.

"Well, actually, it's –" I'm about to tell him my PhD's funded by the Arts and Humanities Research Council, but he cuts me off again.

"Bet your dad would think it was his lucky day if you bagged yourself a man with sixteen acres. Take you off his hands, eh?" He throws back his head and laughs as if he's just said something hilarious.

"My dad's dead," I say.

He has the decency to look slightly mortified at this. "Oh. Sorry. When did he…?"

"January."

"As in, January just past?"

"Three months ago. Yeah." He looks so flummoxed that I actually feel a bit bad about springing it on him. "But I'm fine about it," I add, waving a hand to show how unbothered I am.

"Right. Well, ah…" He takes a long gulp of his pint, and I can see the panicked look in his eyes that people always get when I tell them. "What did he do? Probably had a good pension, did he?"

I stare at him in disbelief. Luckily, at that moment Brendan bursts into the bar with all his usual lack of stealth. He's closely followed by Jude, who's wearing dark sunglasses like she's on some kind of spy mission. They stand there scanning the room for a second before Brendan clocks me and jerks his head in recognition. I cringe and sink lower in my seat, praying he doesn't just barrel over and challenge Trevor to a fight or something. Luckily, though, Jude grabs his sleeve and darts in front of him as they approach the table. "Aoife?" she says sharply. She's using her scary voice. Jude was a policewoman before she left to do her PhD, and she can be really intimidating when she wants to be.

Trevor looks up with a blank expression.

"Hey, guys," I say weakly. As horrible as he is, I can't help feeling a little bit bad for him.

"There's been an emergency," Jude says in the same commanding tone. "We need you to come with us right now."

SAM McNEILLY

Why I Shot the Elephant

Synopsis

Why I Shot the Elephant *follows 27-year-old Guildford resident Noah Webb who, in an attempt to forge a career as a travel vlogger in Pakistan, fakes his own kidnapping. This satirical story opens with a prologue detailing the night of Noah's "kidnapping" from Lahore's Anarkali Bazaar by a masked and mysterious trio who putter off in a battered rickshaw. From there, the novel alternates between main chapters that follow Noah's journey from privileged anonymity to the subject of an international manhunt, and interstitial chapters that offer further insight into Noah's activities through articles, podcast transcripts, social media posts, and other non-narrative media.*

Bored of his comfortable yet monotonous life working for his father's insurance company, Noah finds inspiration from a British-Pakistani Deliveroo rider to establish a career as a travel vlogger. In Pakistan, he begins collaborating with a local group of content producers, with whom he shoots semi-popular and controversial videos across Lahore, Islamabad, Karachi, and Fairy Meadows. Noah's profile captures the attention of a group of white travel vloggers who are rumoured to run a "content sweatshop," and even to have murdered an American rival. They ambush Noah, aiming to blackmail him into partnering with them, but Noah counters with his own proposition: a one-off collaboration in which they fake his kidnapping to garner international media attention and popularity. They agree, but their amateur attempt quickly descends into a frantic flight from Lahore's elite "Dolphin Force" police unit into Kashmir, where British armed forces—who believe the kidnapping to be real—liberate Noah. He returns to Guildford, allowing the blame to fall on his collaborators.

Through a narrative structure that reflects the experience of scrolling through social media, Why I Shot the Elephant *satirises the ways in which digital content producers perpetuate colonial forms of cultural and economic exchange.*

Prologue
That Video

In that moment his three kidnappers bundled him into the back a of a rickshaw, Noah—despite the uncontrollable terror trembling through his muscles—knew the footage would make great content.

That video of Noah Webb, 27-year-old innocent British travel vlogger, being kidnapped from one of the most popular night-markets in Lahore, Pakistan became a global phenomenon. It was reported on, discussed, parodied, memed, gamified, remixed, argued over, and had subtitle translations in over 50 languages.

It was divisive, too. Even in Noah's own family. His mum went on Sky News and demanded tighter border control for Pakistanis. 'These Islamic maniacs were hiding Bin Laden for years, and now they've kidnapped my own son! You want to continue welcoming them to the UK?'

Then, on Channel 4 News came his dad's retort. 'Stricter border control? Leave it to Noah's mother to blame Osama Bin bloody Laden when our son behaves like a fucking idiot. Maybe we need to control him instead.'

During his captivity, if he'd been able to keep track of its view count, he would've taken some consolation from the fact that that video was watched by more people than the last three Strictly finals *combined.* After dreaming of fame, Noah became an international celebrity while chained to a radiator in an old hut somewhere in the foothills of the Himalayas. Pete Davidson played him in an SNL skit. Piers Morgan called him *a resilient English hero*. And then the manhunt kicked off, sending four nuclear-armed states into a diplomatic crisis over his whereabouts.

For different reasons, many people shared that video with a strange satisfaction, as if they'd been proved right about their beliefs.

@CaligulasWetDream: Doesn't he know that's what happens when you visit the Third World? Moron!

@Jackanorydorydoo: I don't even go to Southall alone. Who are these idiots flying to literal hubs of terrorism?

@SimpingMarx: Of course a white man being kidnapped on his poverty safari gets global coverage. Is anyone even interested in the thousands of Muslims being killed every day in senseless wars?

Noah, if he could've seen them, wouldn't have minded all these comments. In fact, he would've enjoyed reading them. But his only focus was escaping captivity unscathed. He knew if he could somehow free himself, and prevent the story of his time in Pakistan from turning into a tragedy, the experience would provide him a platform from which to launch his profile to heights he'd never imagined.

* * *

Although he hadn't been in Pakistan long, Noah had garnered online controversy at the time of his kidnapping. In the weeks leading up to that fateful night, several blog posts and articles had been written about the behaviour of white travel vloggers trying to establish themselves in Pakistan. And, whether fairly or not, for many of these social media commentators Noah served as the most egregious example.

Accusations of Islamophobia, sexism, and profiting off poor people's misery worked to turn some of Noah's budding following—and, crucially, brands—away from him. But, being raised by an entrepreneurial, no-nonsense father, Noah was determined to win them back. Which is why he went to the Anarkali Bazaar night-market, from where he was kidnapped. Ahmed Khan—a local Lahori journalist, and one of Noah's harshest critics—offered him the chance to clear his name after he'd published a scathing appraisal of Noah's activities on his Substack. On his way to meet Ahmed, Noah wondered whether he was being foolish. His dad, Jeffrey Webb, certainly thought he was. In a phone call not long before he left, Jeffrey told Noah it was *like Prince Andrew agreeing to another interview with Emily Maitlis*.

Noah left his hotel that evening harbouring deep concerns about his decision. But viewers couldn't tell that when he began his livestream. Since he'd started receiving criticism, Noah had wisely changed tack in his approach to content. Rather than continuing to post what he deemed light-hearted, funny clips of himself interacting with locals, he'd started to film himself in awe of Pakistan's unique culture.

'Mashallah, brothers and sisters! For my Western viewers, "Mashallah" is an Urdu word that roughly translates as "I appreciate God for giving you good vibes." Come on, peeps—every day is a day to learn something! I am so blessed to be here at the incredible Anarkali Bazaar night-market, and I want to continue showing you all the Pakistan we don't see on the news.'

Noah flipped the camera from his goofily grinning, lightly stubbled, framed-by-bobbing-blonde-locks face to the market's crowded lanes and stalls.

'Here is some of the real beauty of Pakistan. On display for your very eyes. Each stall is exhibiting such rich heritage and skillful craftsmanship–I mean, check out this intricate embroidery, the fabrics, the kurtas.' Noah turned the camera back to himself for a moment, so he could wink and show his audience his own tightly fitting kurta, which he'd livestreamed himself buying after haggling a market owner down to half the originally stated price. 'Which I look damn *foine* in, don't you think? Ha, ha! And man, I just love how they've hung up all these strings of fairy lights over the bustling hive of activity. It's such a vibe, y'know? A Mashallah vibe. I swear I haven't experienced this sort of atmosphere since Isle of Wight Fest 2019.'

'Sahib!' A stall owner called to Noah.

'You hear that, peeps? "Sahib" is a term of utmost respect for men.'

'Sahib, apsay mill kur pata chala hai kay goray bhi gareeb aur kanjoos hotay hain.'

'Thank you, brother!' Noah turned back to his viewers. 'I get called Sahib all the time over here, and not just by hopeful salesmen. Pakistanis are so kind. And gracious.'

Noah reached the end of the row of clothing stalls and entered a square lined by food vendors. The air grew smokey. All around, a variety of kababs, karahi, biryani, chaats, haleem, and so many more dishes were being cooked and served.

'Oh, good God, the food! Honestly, my favourite thing about Pakistan is its food. Check all this out—they have so many colourful dishes, and they all have such foreign aromas and diverse flavours which just... Remember those mini Chicken Kiev balls you'd get as a kid? Well, every dish is like eating *exotic*, mini Chicken Kiev balls. The flavours just burst in your mouth.' Noah's zoomed his camera past the customers and vendors and through a gap in two food stalls to focus on a KFC. 'Even the KFC over here is insane. They do these things called masala fries which are spicy AF! They will blow. your. mind. And the Zinger Towers—trust me when I say you've never had a chicken burger with seasoning like they do here in Pakistan. How am I going to return to the UK and eat stodgy fish 'n' chips and rubbery pork pies?'

Noah turned the camera back on himself, ready to deliver one of the reflective summaries that he'd been practising in recent streams. He felt that, in his short time in Pakistan, he'd seriously matured. No longer would he seek cheap laughs that, *yes*, he was willing to admit, *might occur at the expense of the less fortunate*. He was after a new audience, one that was more serious, refined, *learnéd.* He planned to branch out from social media, see if he could land himself a reputable role—maybe he could be a millennial Michael Palin, a more jocular Joanna Lumley, a less deranged Neil Oliver.

'Listen, brothers, sisters, future exes... sharing all this with you, I'm just so appreciative to God and Steve Jobs for technology, y'know? Social media, this phone, sure, they have their issues, but they've also allowed me—an average guy—to bring the real Pakistan to you. Live. Can you imagine when people visited these places back in the day, and all they could do was write about it? Like, an entire book? And people would have to read hundreds of words, just so they can imagine exotic lands—not even see them! Man, life must've been so depressing back then. No entertainment. No experiences. Just you and your mind, trying to think about stuff. And look, Pakistan, it's showed me a different way of life. Sure, it doesn't have those creature comforts that make life in the UK much more enjoyable. I mean, did you know Pret still hasn't opened a branch here? How insane is that? There's literally Prets opening next door to other Prets in the UK. Plus, another thing I've noticed, despite the intense, crushing poverty, they don't even have an equivalent of Tesco Meal Deals or Meerkat Movies.' Noah gave his trademark cheeky grin to camera. 'Mr Tesco: DM me. I think I've found a new market for you. Ha, ha! No but really, despite all the challenges the Pakistani people face, they have such big hearts. And I guess a lot of that comes from the country's sense of spirituality, which is highly infectious... like laughter, not disease—before any of you jokers take my words out of context again! And, I know a lot of you are curious about my religion after I posted my shahada. But listen, my faith's a private matter. Oh!'

Noah looked past the camera to someone he recognised.

'Here he is! The great canceller! Ahmed Khan: judge, jury, and executioner of South Asian social media.'

The camera flipped to show Ahmed. He wore a creased white t-shirt, black cardigan, jeans, and sneakers. His unruly, long curly hair hung around his bespectacled face, a bushy beard covering his chin.

'Noah. We agreed no filming until we're in the podcast studio.'

'He's such a grump, this lad! What's the matter, Ahmed? Did you stain your favourite Metallica shirt?'

'Noah, I really—'

'Oh, I'm just messing, you big grubby bear! Listen, guys—'

Noah's words were cut out by the screech of tyres. The camera swerved. A rickshaw had stopped on the side of the road, right in front of Noah and Ahmed. In it were three masked figures.

* * *

Before they'd even jumped out of the rickshaw, Noah knew they were after him. In the back of his head for the previous weeks, he'd wondered if something like this might happen. Through the social media beef he'd been embroiled in, so much information about him had been leaked: his earnings from brand deals, who he'd been meeting with, the expensive equipment he used, and, crucially, his travel itinerary.

As one of the most prominent of a very limited number of white travel vloggers in Pakistan, his dad strenuously warned him to keep as low a profile as possible. *You're standing out like a Bentley in Blackpool!*

A deep sense of regret swelled in Noah when he clocked the headbands each kidnapper wore. *Black Arabic writing on a white background.* It didn't matter that Noah had no idea what the writing said—on reflection, he realised tweeting *the Pakistani Taliban are inbred incels* (and tagging the group's main account, @TehrikiTalibPak07) as a way to seem edgy and funny, probably wasn't his smartest idea.

From the first flash of their Kalashnikovs, Ahmed bolted. Noah called after him, his words quivering with fear.

'Alright, Ahmed! Just run off, yeah? I thought you said it's a journalist's job to run *towards* danger?'

For the most fleeting of moments, Noah exchanged silent glances with his kidnappers. He looked at them. They looked at him. Then, one of the trio screamed at him, in what he assumed was Urdu, but what was actually Punjabi (in a previous livestream, a Pakistani viewer had tried to explain the intricacies of the many languages spoken throughout the country, to which Noah responded *Ah, so Punjabi is a type of Urdu, sort of like how Scouse is its own version of English*). Noah's monolingualism wasn't a problem in this situation, though. He easily inferred what they were communicating.

Get in the rickshaw. Now.

Noah, not wanting to give in to their demands so easily, sought clarification.

'Woah! What is it, mate? I only speak English.'

Suddenly, an idea popped into Noah's mind. What if I pray? He wondered if that would be problematic. He'd faced some harsh criticisms after livestreaming his conversion to Islam. But surely, when armed figures are trying to kidnap him, he couldn't be criticised for seeking help from a higher power? There was only one problem: he had no idea how to pray. Plus, a guy who said he was a Muslim scholar had told Noah that Allah doesn't prioritise the prayers of women, gay people, or *goras*.

'Brother, if you fall into one of these categories, you first need to build up loyalty points with the almighty to have a prayer answered.' *So like how you get your tenth coffee free at Caffè Nero*, Noah thought to himself.

Prayer obviously wasn't the answer. But he sought a way to stall further.

'Listen, please explain what you mean in English.'

Despite feeling like his bowels were on the brink of a major evacuation—partly from fear, and partly from the remnants of an undercooked goat kebab he'd had the previous night—he said it slowly and clearly. Later, Noah's dad nearly burst a blood vessel after reading a commenter on a *Guardian* article pointing out that it's "condescending" and "behaviour typical of an English tourist" to speak to "residents of the Global South" in that tone. *White men have to be woke even when they're pleading with people trying to abduct them,* he raged silently.

In response to Noah's request for clarity, all three of his kidnappers shouted at him, before collectively dragging him towards the rickshaw.

Noah noted that, as it'd been almost two months since he'd stepped foot in a David Lloyd, his core strength had dwindled, so his ability to resist was limited. And then he received an infamous sucker punch which reverberated through his skull (and then, thanks to the livestream, around the world) to momentarily stun him. The kidnappers proceeded to stuff him in the back of their rickshaw like an awkward sleeping bag refusing to fit in its sack when packing up at the end of a festival.

In the struggle, he briefly managed to hold onto his phone, which was still streaming. He knew this was his last chance to get a message out.

'Guys! This is no joke! These people are kidnapping me! Please, contact someone who can rescue me—the British embassy, the SAS, Richard Branson! Anyone who can get me out of here. Help me!'

His plea ended there. His kidnappers wrested his phone and tossed it from the speeding rickshaw. Noah's feed remained on for a few minutes, quietly watching the hazy glow of the Moon as it tried to pierce the thick smog that hangs over Lahore. And then *that* video ends.

TERRI MULLHOLLAND

The House of Lost Threads

Synopsis

A haunted house tale about three generations of women who disappear. When MAGGIE is born, MOTHER is hospitalised with post-natal psychosis. Maggie and her older sister LUCY are cared for by GRANDMA until Maggie is four. Maggie has no memory of this time or Grandma. She is told Grandma disappeared and was never seen again. Mother leaves hospital and they move to a new house. Mother suffers a miscarriage, witnessed by Maggie, and returns to hospital. DAD says Mother's coming home soon. She never does. Shortly after, Lucy disappears, leaving behind her red coat. Maggie and Dad pretend Lucy is at home sick. Maggie plays along because Lucy has become her imaginary friend. When Dad dies Maggie finds the key to Grandma's. Dad kept this secret all her life.

The taxi driver who drops Maggie at Grandma's tells her the house refused to burn. Inside, is Maggie's imaginary sister Lucy. And Grandma – who is alive, half-crazy (she hears voices from the house), and living in the cellar of the house – terrified of the house's other inhabitants.

The house is the keeper of memories and projects them to Maggie – Mother and the baby she lost live in the attic. The same attic Grandma kept Maggie and Lucy (after receiving instructions from the house). Maggie discovers Mother never came home because she attempted to kill herself and Lucy. By the end, Maggie suspects she succeeded and Dad kept it from her. Now the house wants Maggie to join them and live happily ever after. The taxi driver's mother tells Maggie the villagers set fire to Grandma's house because they believed it was possessed by evil. When they learn the ghosts are back they return. Lucy warns Maggie and as the fire rages, Maggie follows Lucy in her red coat through the woods.

Once upon a time, at different times, there were three women who walked out of their homes and never came back.

There was a little girl in a red coat, a Mother who left a trail of blood, and a Grandma who never made it into town.

Once upon a time there was a woman who tried to follow all these lost threads home.

Chapter 1

Maggie arrived the day before January's full wolf moon. The night when wolves howl the loudest.

Outside the station, a short man in dark glasses was leaning against his cab, smoking a cigarette.

'Where to?' he asked in the familiar West Country accent of her childhood.

Maggie gave him the address, printed in capitals on a piece of paper in Mother's best writing. He took off his glasses, peered at it, peered at her.

'They call it the house that refused to burn,' he dropped the cigarette and ground it into the tarmac with his heel. 'That place has been derelict for years. What business you got there?'

Maggie covered her discomfort at this challenge with false bravado. 'It was my grandma's house.' She dug into her pocket and held up a set of keys. 'It's mine now.'

'Is it now?' He put his glasses back on so she couldn't read his expression. 'Get in then.'

He drove her in silence out of the town, past farms and woodland. When he spoke his voice made her jump. 'You planning on moving in there?'

She shrugged, avoiding his face in the rear-view mirror. 'Guess I'll see what it's like first.'

'It's not somewhere you want to stay. Teenagers round here, they used to dare each other to go up and ring the bell.' He paused long enough for her to look at him in the mirror. 'They stopped doing that after someone answered. That poor young girl was never the same again.'

'Who was it? Who answered?'

'She was never able to say. Someone came and boarded it up after that. Reckon it was the same person who tried to set fire to it. But it refused to burn.'

'Probably just kids messing about,' said Maggie. She hoped she sounded dismissive, like she didn't care.

'Whoever started that fire, it wasn't kids. And whatever stopped it burning. Well, let's just say that wasn't kids either.'

They got to the top of a narrow lane and the taxi driver stopped, refusing to go any further. 'Not been a vehicle down there in years. I'll never get her back out.'

'I can't see the house?'

'It'll be there,' said the driver.

Their fingers touched briefly as she handed him the ten-pound note and he gave a slight smirk.

Maggie adjusted her small rucksack and made her way down the overgrown track. There was a buzzing from the electricity pylons in the field beyond and the air smelled like the day after Bonfire Night: acrid, sulphuric. She glanced over her shoulder – the taxi driver was watching her. But by the time the house came into sight she heard the revving of an engine and he was gone.

She was already regretting taking a taxi all the way here. They'd passed a new estate about a mile or so back, she could have got him to drop her there. And why did she have to mention Grandma? He was bound to talk to someone. She knew what small towns were like.

I dropped someone at that house – said she was the granddaughter.

There'd be people in the town who remembered or who'd heard the stories. They'd all be on the doorstep the next day on the pretence of asking if she was okay and if there was anything she needed. But really wanting the gossip.

There had always been gossip about the family. Tales as tall as anything she made up and she made up a lot.

She always had a story, was always the storyteller.

The house had that unhappy look of long forgotten places: weary, exhausted. Dead ivy pockmarked the walls, browning like old scabs. The front garden was overgrown; an army of stinging nettles protected the path along with coils of bramble like barbed wire. An ash tree lay fallen across the lawn: an extra barricade. The weeds looked like the only living thing to touch the house in some time. Everything else looked dead. Or maybe not quite dead, just hibernating, biding its time.

It didn't look like a real house. Even up close it looked like it was getting ready to disappear – like Grandma, like Mother, like Lucy. It had the discomforting familiarity of places visited often in bad dreams. And she had a lot of bad dreams.

Wooden boards covered the downstairs windows and the front door. Those over the front door were blackened and the scorch marks extended past the boards along one side darkening the Cotswold stone all the way to the attic. The taxi driver was right – *the house that refused to burn.*

Something about that story was familiar, some hazy memory from long ago. It wasn't the first time she'd heard it. Everything she knew about Grandma was gleaned from scraps of overheard conversations between her parents, rumours from various babysitters, telephone calls late at night. Her and Lucy, lying on their tummies, peering through the banisters on the first-floor landing of the New House when they should have been in bed – listening.

The boards looked like an amateur job, flimsy timber nailed directly onto the wooden door and window frames. Nothing like the proper metal security screens she saw along the North Circular in London, with their lines of rivets sealing out the light.

Looks were deceiving, as she should have known. The letterbox was uncovered and Maggie tried pulling at the board above it, where she imagined the key hole might be, but it held fast. The wood was old, but the nails were shiny and new. Not such an amateur job.

Maggie slammed her palm into the door. Why hadn't she thought of this? Now she was miles from anywhere with no way of getting into the one place for which she had the keys.

What did she expect? That she'd just walk up the garden path and open the door? Maybe she expected Grandma would be there waiting for her with a nice cup of tea and a slice of cake? Just what had she expected?

Lucy. Maybe she'd expected Lucy.

Nobody knew what happened to the women in her family. Nobody ever told her where they went or why she and Dad pretended for so long that they were still there.

Maggie never knew if she'd walk into a shop or a café, or get on a train, or visit a new place, and see her mother or her sister, Lucy.

And as for Grandma, she was either dead, or she was here, in this house – waiting.

Chapter 2

The side gate was unlocked and opened onto a long thin garden, wild and weed-choked. A grey stone face peered at Maggie from the top of a crumbling fountain – fractured and blistered with lichen, giving it the malevolent snarl of a fallen angel.

Less effort had been made on the security boards on the back door; they came away with such unexpected ease that Maggie staggered backwards, narrowly avoiding a clump of nettles. The key slid into the lock as if it was in regular use, but the door was swollen with damp and needed a hefty kick before it opened in a series of stutters, grinding grit on the tiled floor.

A dank, mouldy smell hit her as she entered the tiny hallway. Brushing away the cobwebs that hung like torn net curtains from the ceiling, Maggie shivered. She'd never been good with spiders or other creatures that liked to inhabit abandoned houses – another thing she hadn't thought of when she came up with this crazy plan.

She brushed against a dark woollen jacket, hanging from a hook, releasing a flurry of moths and a soft scream.

Deep breath. She needed to calm down. She hadn't even got past the hall yet.

The inner door was propped open with an iron boot scraper – leading to what Mother would have called the scullery – and there was a scurrying and scuttling of creatures as they hid from the vibrations of her feet. The place was probably infested with rats and mice and God knew what. Maggie left the back door open for air and light and, although she didn't articulate it fully in her head, an easy escape.

On the shelves in the scullery were tins and packets of things, all gathering dust and dead flies. Tucked beneath a low bench was a pair of tartan slippers waiting for their owner to slip them on; the toes worn or eaten away.

The floor was tiled with brown and beige patterned tiles: straight lines leading to a circle in the middle. A sudden mental image of a small hand pushing a toy car around the circle; pretending it was a roundabout and the lines were roads. There was another hand, also a child's hand, but bigger than the one on the car. She couldn't be sure if the other hand was trying to take the toy away or helping her keep to the lines.

Don't go off the road, Maggie. Don't go off the rails.

Was that Lucy's voice? It was so faint. But what would she be doing here?

Maggie was told she never went to Grandma's, in the same way she was told her mother was coming home soon: with averted eyes, shifting hands, and that habit her dad had of biting and picking at the skin around his nails, tearing cuticles to blood.

Now, she felt the house tense around her, holding its breath, waiting to see what she would do, what she would remember.

It started with the keys – discovered after Dad's death a month ago. They were hidden in Mother's bureau, in the secret bit at the back where nineteenth-century ladies concealed love letters. A single brown envelope marked *Mother* in Mother's writing – Mother's mother, Maggie's grandma. Two keys, on a keyring made from a hard circle of leather embossed with the letter R, wrapped up in an address. It was the only thing her mother left that felt like any kind of clue.

But it started long before then, two decades ago, in the seventies, when first Grandma, then Mother and then Maggie's sister Lucy took it in turns to disappear. All that time she thought Dad was searching and not finding them, but he'd had the keys all along.

She wasn't faultless in this. She knew that. The last few years, even before Dad was ill, hadn't been one long investigation. Most of the time Maggie forgot about them. It was such a long time ago and she was so young when it happened; she'd never really known what it was like to have a Mother and she'd never known Grandma. Even Lucy faded after a while – leaving her as an only child with a single parent. It was always Maggie and Dad against the world. But now, it was as if Dad's death had woken her up from a dream.

Because wasn't the truth that she and Dad deliberately didn't search for them?

Her father was the figure who remained consistent in Maggie's life. When he died, he was the only one in the family whose whereabouts could legally be verified. Not only did she have the official death certificate, she saw the body in the coffin, witnessed it being lowered into the ground. There was a headstone marking the plot that she could visit. Of course, that was only the site of his physical remains, she knew that. His spirit may well be roaming free around the world – but her father was the only one who didn't haunt her. Maybe because he was the only one who was really dead.

When Maggie cleared out his house to return it to the council she found the keys and not much else – no photographs, no letters – no evidence at all that he'd ever had a wife and children. There was no marriage certificate and no birth certificates for her and Lucy. He kept nothing from their childhood either, no school reports or certificates. Nothing, apart from one drawing she did at playschool before it all happened, and that was so well hidden she almost missed it.

To Maggie, it was like she'd disappeared too. Like her childhood never happened. Like it was all just one big story and there was nobody left now who could tell her the beginning, the middle, or the end.

The scullery led down a long corridor to the front of the house and into the kitchen: all dark wood, musty and rotten. The single window was boarded up from the outside, but there was a gap slightly higher than her eyes, that shone a crack of light into the room. Standing on tiptoe she had a clear sightline, all the way down the track. A spyhole to keep watch. *I spy with my little eye*. Someone could have stood here and watched her making her way up the track, watched her walk around to the back of the house. Plenty of time to run and hide. *Ready or not, here I come*.

There was an old-fashioned, cast-iron cooking range, and an absence of white goods in the kitchen. No fridge or freezer or washing machine, and no spaces where they should have been. On the draining board, a teacup was turned upside down next to a saucer and teaspoon. A last cup of tea.

She hadn't realised it would be like this, like the owner had just stepped out, leaving everything behind. She'd assumed it would all be packed up, tidied away – although by whom she couldn't say – leaving behind an empty space for her to walk into, to replace Grandma. To disappear.

KATE PACKMAN

You Can See the End of the World From Here

Synopsis

Vivian, menopausal and separated, is off work with stress-induced insomnia. She rediscovers a journal entry reminding her that her son, Jake, prophesised he would die before turning twelve. The novel counts down to his 12th birthday.

Despite sleeping tablets and therapy, her insomnia worsens as she obsesses over how Jake might die. Scout leaders and teachers become predators. Jake confesses to being unwell. Vivian catastrophises. Meanwhile her neighbours worry her. Warring newly-weds, Hugh and Leanne, live opposite and she witnesses them argue. Malcolm next door, walks his dog at all hours and is a keen bird watcher. She reframes this as predatory behaviour towards Jake. She keeps Jake off school, uses a psychic, increases her sleeping tablets and cuts off Jake's dad.

Jake attends a scout trip and Vivian explores the local beach at night. She bumps into Malcolm who notices her pyjamas and that she left her door open. Malcolm calls round to check on Jake making her more suspicious.

Jake's blood tests are clear, fuelling her accident/predator theory. She witnesses another violent argument between Hugh and Leanne. She increases her sleeping tablets again, records her neighbours' movements, barricades her front door, unplugs the landline. She argues with Jake. He runs away. Malcolm finds him and brings him home.

Vivian pretends Jake's school trip to France is cancelled. To hide him they go wild camping. She buys drugs to keep herself alert. Unhappy with no Wi-Fi Jake is desperate to go home. Her stimulant drugs run out, so she drugs Jake with her sleeping tablets. Jake discovers what she has done and runs away. He fetches the emergency services. Vivian is hospitalised. She has a vivid dream about Jake's birth and nearly dies. The story ends with Jake surviving his birthday and Vivian receiving the help she needs/in recovery.

Mark the water not far out to sea,
Fourteen hundred tonnes of high explosives,
Buried in the belly of its liberty
Snapped in half on the sands beyond all help,
The truth of it – this wartime souvenir,
Is common knowledge but whisper to yourself that,
you can see the end of the world from here.
(Sheerness Sea Defences, Isle of Sheppey)

41 Days

1.23 a.m.
I scrunch my eyes closed and will my son's words to disappear from the page. I could let my tears wash them away, yet I know it's too late for me. I'll never forget I've read them. I can only hope they don't come true.

Pulling my dad's cardigan tight around my shoulders, I sniff at the wool, pushing my glasses up my nose at the same time. I haven't washed it since he died and the smell of him comforts me. My shoulders heave again. *Deep breaths, Viv. Smell the soup; cool the soup*. I'd read that in a book once and the advice stayed with me. It had made my therapist laugh but the funny side is lost on me tonight. Another tear drop falls onto the page of my journal so before I lose the words, I dab at the salty puddle with my cardigan sleeve. The frayed wool stops the ink bleeding into the weave of the paper.

At my last therapy session my counsellor, Phil, suggested therapeutic writing might help control my symptoms and improve my mood. I'd told him about my old journals. *Re-reading past entries from when your life was more positive might help you gain perspective, Vivian*.

'Well that back-fired, didn't it Phil?'

My curated collection of journals line my bookshelf on the landing. I had followed Phil's instructions and looked for something to re-read. Disregarding my childhood scribblings, buried in the loft space with my teenage journals and my geography A-level coursework (I can't bring myself to throw out the curled pages of my coastal erosion project), I searched through the ones I'd written in the last eleven years. I'd skipped past the one when I was pregnant (whilst carrying Jake I didn't blossom or bloom or any of the things people promise you) and the most recent one which was all about Dave. The journal had to feature Jake though. Only Jake matters now.

Why did it have to be *that* journal I reopened?

I cover Jake's words with my fingers.

We'd been sat around the caravan table; the Spanish spring weather having let us down for the second day in a row. With a game of Happy

Families underway, I quizzed our six-year-old son about what he wanted to be when he grew up. A baker? A police officer? A pilot? He hadn't hesitated to answer.

It doesn't matter, Mum. I'm only going to live 'til I'm twelve.

Dave laughed at Jake's morbid prophecy. Fear struck me like a slap across the face. Later that night, I wrote down his words, verbatim. If only I'd laughed too.

Jake's prophecy travels through my fingertips and scores itself into my mind with the permanence of a stonemason marking a grave. I close my journal and place it in my pocket. Pulling the cardigan tighter, I try to remember what my dad's hugs felt like.

While I relive Jake's words, my mum and son are in bed with their bellies full of greasy fish and chips. *Grandma's treat,* she cooed, *it'll be a while until we get to share a Sunday night takeaway again.* I tried to tempt my small family unit with Chinese food but I'd been outnumbered. I file the out of date takeaway menu back on the kitchen side, setting it between a letter pleading with me to insure my water pipes and a rather early invitation from Saga to subscribe to old age. Rude. I catch sight of Jake's school trip letter. Over dinner he had shown his grandma the itinerary for his residential visit to Normandy. It means he will be in France for his birthday. I pull the letter towards me. An official-looking A4 envelope, thick and high-quality compared to the school photocopy, comes with it. I push it away.

On bright summer days, if we stand on the beach and squint, we can catch a glimpse of France. Yet, when I imagine him there alone, it could be 20,000 leagues under the sea, not twenty miles across the Channel. Scout camp next week – on the island – feels doable but France? My chest tightens and the tears restart. I won't be able to protect him in France and he's twelve in forty-one days.

Forty-one days.

It's only forty-one days 'til my birthday! Jake's innocent countdown at breakfast had sounded as ominous as the sunken munitions deep inside *SS Richard Montgomery*. A ticking bomb. Mum's disapproval rings in my ears. *I've no idea why you continue to live so near the coast and that ship.* She'd never understood my connection to the sea. Not that it would make any difference where we were on the island if that lot exploded. Folding the itinerary, I use it to bury my divorce papers, shoving them both into my unruly filing system.

1.49 a.m.

Creeping onto the landing, I pause and listen for my mum's deep, nasal snoring. It's so unladylike that I can never bring myself to tell her how bad it sounds. I hope the cabin on her cruise ship has thick walls, or that the passengers are as deaf as her. I sympathise with other insomniacs. Through Jake's open door, I can see the shadow of his hand dangling over the side of his bed, his solar system duvet barely covering him. I must update his bedding to something more age-appropriate soon, though it will have to wait until I'm back at work on full pay.

The only family I have left sleep soundly, making me jealous. Mum's snores rumble in time with the rolling waves lapping at the base of Minster Cliffs. My room, without Dave keeping the bed warm, looks uninviting. Empty. The beach will be empty too. Better to wander over the sands of an unspoilt coastline than toss and turn in bed. I tuck the greying strands of my unruly bob, too many to yank out now, behind my ears, and grab my navy coat off the banister to go over my Dad's cardigan.

2.19 a.m.
The wet sand tries to swallow my feet as small waves lap at the strandline. The earlier high tide mark, littered with tangled bladderwrack and the odd mermaid's purse, catches the moonlight. I walk along its edge. My mum used to moan at my untidy collection of dogfish cases. When I lived at home, the bathroom windowsill was littered with ocean detritus: rows of razor shells, crabs' discarded claws and one starfish (all appendages intact). The starfish now hangs on my bathroom wall between the dangly light pull and the mirror bordered with shell fragments. Dave had bought the mirror for me at the Shellness craft fair. He'd seen me fall in love with it and then walk away because of the price tag. He'd crept back, bought it and surprised me later that night by pulling it from under my pillow like a magician. Pebbles and pieces of driftwood – anything shaped by the sea's fists – still catch my eye, but I let Jake do the cataloguing and displaying these days. My own ambitions of being a marine biologist are long buried.

I drag my shoe through the sand, making a deep groove to match the lines that furrow my brow. I stretch out my forehead trying to smooth the lines away. I check the time: 2.30 a.m. My mum leaves for her cruise in a few hours. Two months around the Med. Sixty days.

She won't be here if it happens.

I'm glad she spent her last night on the island with us. I know it's her way of checking up on me but it also meant she saw her grandson one last time before his birthday. Jake had spent all evening grilling her for details of this 'once in a lifetime' trip. *The ship will be full, Jakey. I'll be able to wander out of my cabin, day or night, and there'll be someone on deck, or in one of the restaurants. There's every nationality of food. French delicacies one night, Thai the next. There's even a cinema on board!* Jake's eyes had widened at the thought of twenty-four-hour restaurants and free movies. He had speculated he might be eating croissants in France at the same time as she would be eating them on board her cruise ship. I should let him go to France. In the distance, the lights from a cruise liner sit on the horizon. My shoulders quiver as I shake off the thought of Jake crossing the sea without me.

Of him being trapped on a ferry with crowds of people.

Of him not being able to escape.

Crowds are becoming a problem for me. The more time I spend off work, the fewer people I see, the less I want company. Last night, my mum had teased me, *You're like a hermit. A hermit crab hiding in your house, and crotchety too.* She had snorted at her little joke and elbowed Jake in the ribs. I didn't laugh: her jibe stung. When dad had died, she retreated inward. Dave hadn't died; he'd left. But both equalled loss. Both hurt. I miss my dad more than Dave. I pull at his cardigan under my coat – folding myself between the swathes of wool that had been needed to reach around his expansive waistline. I'm still too angry with Dave to miss him.

Thought about going back to work, have you Vivian? Subtle as a sea wall my mum.

A ringed plover scuttles past, flashing black and white feathers as it splashes through the water's edge. It stops to wade the shallows and search for worms. I check my watch again, the cracked face reminding me of another expense I can't afford.

I had tried returning to work.

Humiliation flushes my cheeks. I rub my hands across my face, reshaping the skin to erase the shame. On the first day back after the summer break, I'd sat at one of the school desks, listening to a group of pupils share their holiday experiences. The teacher had hoped the new initiative of talking through their ideas before writing might help them put words on the page. My knees skimmed the underneath of the table. The pupils' pencil cases gleamed with the potential of a new school year. One of the pupils held everyone's attention as he announced his parents were getting a divorce. He had boasted about getting two holidays, described his two bedrooms, but I could see the pain behind his eyes. I tried to keep my emotions in check but the way his voice cracked, it broke me. Full sobs and angry tears had scourged my face. The pupils stared, mouths hanging open as I ran to the bathroom, mortified.

Obviously my mum thought I should try again. I had shut her down with a dark look and tucked back into the fish and chip supper I didn't even want. I won't discuss my anxieties in front of Jake. He's seen enough of my breakdown and heard enough about his dad being to blame.

Work, and Dave's absence, seem the least of my problems now. The scrawled words in my journal weigh me down like the stones Jake collects from the beach, bulging in my pockets until the fabric of my cardigan stretches, changing shape until they resemble monstrous growths. Tonight, I considered telling my mum about Jake's morbid prophecy, but when they both went to bed at the same time, my mum announcing *I need my beauty sleep*, the moment never arrived. The words, like the fossils on Warden Point beach, stay buried inside me.

It's better I don't tell her.

Worrying about me and Jake will spoil my mum's longed-for holiday. The first holiday she has been brave enough to go on alone. And although I know a flippant dismissal of six-year-old Jake's words will follow my confession, my mum will nevertheless worry. She won't understand my fear. She won't acknowledge it. Phil's plea for me to *talk more, Vivian* does not apply here. My mum needs me to be okay, so she can enjoy herself. Have I managed to hide my escalating insomnia? Hanging around on the beach in the early hours of the morning might not help my case. I must get back before they wake.

I run my fingers through my hair. It needed a wash before and now salt tangles the strands together. Lack of sleep pulls at my face. Will my eyes betray me? Will each burst blood vessel reveal another broken night? As I climb the cliff path, passing the sea lavender and the pink daisies of the sea asters, I pinch my cheeks for colour. I will blame my red eyes on the early morning walk, a result of the sea spray and the sand-filled breeze coming off the water.

Once my mum leaves the island and boards the train for Southampton, I can relax again. Stop pretending I'm okay. Jake won't ask any questions. He doesn't want to know about my problems. A bit more time and my group therapy sessions will help. I shake out my limbs and start to head home. Once I can put the journal entry behind me, once I can convince myself not to believe six-year-old Jake and his dark prophecy, I will sleep better.

REJINA SABUR-CROSS

Between the Silence and the Sound

Synopsis

*It's Easter 2015 and **Jamie** (white) reluctantly introduces newly-pregnant **Salima** (brown) to his emphatically unwoke family in their remote Somerset village.*

*She's vaguely aware of their xenophobia, but Jamie's hoping they've changed. Neither know **Danny** (far-right eco-cult member), his sister's boyfriend, who'll also join. The slow reveal of how their Pagan traditions have become stained with racism, ensues. Macro and micro aggressions clash as family secrets bleed out over the roast, culminating in a terrible act of violence; when a knife's pressed to a neck.*

Part 1

We open into bedlam, around the Payne dining table. A knife's clutched to a throat, but who's and why?

Flashback to Salima's mother: a teenage immigrant in 70's London suffering domestic violence. Her struggle's contrasted with Danny's suburban childhood.

As Salima and Jamie travel to the countryside his anxiety's interwoven with her naïve anticipation.

Part 2

Upon arrival Salima's treated with hostility. Meanwhile, Danny's become a guard at a migrant detention centre. Embittered, he thinks the only path is extremism.

Salima's background also unfurls, via the 90s London Indie scene. An impoverished Muslim female with a Jewish best friend and a violent, antisemitic father; she's forged in the fires of relentless rebellion.

Part 3

Danny arrives for lunch and letches over Salima, enrages Jamie and proposes to Lisa. Jamie announces the pregnancy; and emotions apex.

Interspersed are scenes of Salima's aunts warmly welcoming Jamie.

Back at the family feast, Salima's drugged. Hallucinating she finds Danny's wallet carrying photos of trafficked children.

Festen meets 7even, as the vile reality of who he is sinks home. She clutches the blade to Danny's throat.

Despite Danny's goading to submit to her basest urges, Jamie talks her down. She's saved by the very cultural values they fear. They leave – ultimately stronger than any of them.

SPAFFING – April 5th 2015

When it happens, when the blade is brandished against that delicate throat, there's a shocked bark of laughter and red wine gets spaffed across the freshly-bleached tablecloth.

This of course sets a certain someone off, even though we all know *they've* sliced through more jugulars than our accumulated hot proverbials.

No one would ever describe a Payne get together as "normal", but when the knife is grabbed from the cake stand and a head's yanked back, everyone around the table (bar the hysterical one) is stunned into silence.

For a mad second it looks like they might be going in for a kiss, but instead the metal's positioned along the windpipe, which is all wrong of course, it needs to be moved to the right a bit and at more of an acute angle to really sever the vein, but anyway the whole thing happens so fast that before any of it sinks in everyone around the table just freezes, gobs well and truly smacked. Everyone apart from the howler, who's just sat there cracking up into the absorbent wad of pre-shock.

I mean, to be fair, they're all a bit pissed by this point.

Only moments before, Peter had been explaining his reasons for circling Eid on the family calendar ('because we all need to remain extra vigilant around their festivals, what with all the poaching of late').

Talking over him as always, Janet was saying how '*despite* all the mithering about colonialism and whatnot, everybody forgets don't they, how incredibly tolerant that same Empire's made our great country. Why, if it wasn't for the Colonies we'd never have bestowed our railways, our civilisation on those poor, backwards tribes and just look at how in return we picked up some of your exotic ways, made them our national dish no less, so it's all worked out hasn't it, isn't that right now Sally?" Salima had smiled politely, blinking over at Jamie.

"Of course, nobody's allowed to talk about it anymore are we?" Aunty Gill had said mournfully topping Lisa up. "I mean, if you look at how divided say China and India are, when you think about it, we're not all that bad now are we?" She'd also smiled tenderly at her nephew, but Jamie had glared down at his slice of Simnel as though it had done him a grievance.

"And look at how welcoming your own parents have been!" she'd cooed, going to prop an elbow on the table but missing and almost concussing herself instead. "Opening their arms and front door to all and sundry from every corner of the globe." Jamie had gazed up at the stag's head nailed to the wall, looked deeply into the maudlin mirror of its eyes and said nothing.

It's only been a year but he's obviously forgotten that this is what they do, what they've always done, his family. They like a bit of a drink, a bit of a laugh and then it's putting the world to rights and sod the miserable killjoys who want to rob them of their freedom of speech.

It's been a year since he was last here, a year since he realised his world view was widening at the same pace as theirs appeared to be shrivelling and a year since he stormed out and vowed never to speak to them again. In addition to the twelve month silent treatment, he's decided to flaunt his disdain for them in the most provocative manner possible. By bringing home the very thing they fear the most. Not only bringing one into the house, but actually inviting one to the table to join their 'Eostre' feast, to sleep in his childhood bed. This, his defiantly woke, dark-skinned, neon-haired, proudly Muslim up-the-duff two fingers to the lot of them. Well, of course things were always going to get lairy.

* * *

The tines of a fork pause mid-way to a mouth as eyes bulge stupidly. Seated opposite, a face lights up, almost beatifically. Rubbing elbows with them, someone else pales, as though confronted with an apparition along with the realisation that it's the family carving knife, the precious Athame dagger so carefully sharpened mere hours ago that's being wielded.

The family heirloom, the grain of its handle softened by the sturdy clutches of generations of Paynes, which moments earlier had sliced through the cake Jamie's mum, Janet had lovingly baked and iced and before that through the grain and against the fibres of a good old fashioned roast (not to mention all the other things it's faithfully sliced into).

As vino spatters all over the pristine cloth, everyone else just sits there transfixed as the dark red bubbles up on the weft and warp of cotton, pausing for a second as though even the alcoholic droplets can't quite comprehend the terrible dramatic violence of it all, before sinking in.

As the macabre reality is finally driven home, that a dagger is being held to a throat here at the family table, that there's a time and a place and that even by their standards, this is a step too far, that someone could get arrested and that wine will be an absolute bugger to get out; the howls of hysteria rise to a crescendo as stained crevices are temporarily ironed out, as lips stretch wide and as the bedlam erupts.

As the dam of astonishment splinters and as all hell finally breaks loose.

SALIMA – 24 hours earlier

Salima unpauses the podcast and the tragedy of the Batavia seeps through the air. There's a certain ritualistic calm in having everything laid out; turmeric stained chopping board, dripping colander of spinach, onions, garlic, flour, cumin, chilli flakes, kefir. A puddle of olive oil shimmers in the pan and she imagines the set of a cookery show, instead of their tiny Tottenham kitchen where she stands barefoot in in Jamie's hoody.

Drawing the blade through the sharpener, she begins losing herself in the terrible acts committed by Dutch seamen all those centuries ago. There's a mindlessness to crackling off the skins before carefully dicing each onion, a quiet joy released with every press of the blade.

This is her peaceful place.

As she turns the knife upside down to sizzle the alliums into the pan she tries not to dwell on the nails-down-a-blackboard time she'd caught Jamie cheerfully blunting her favourite Global.

Half listens to the hiss and bloom as the cumin and chilli joins them. Half listens to how quickly the survivors slid into evil. How easily they'd been manipulated to murder; at first for survival and then, apparently for sheer pleasure.

As things begin to caramelise, she shakes a soft hillock of flour from the crumpled bag into a chipped Pyrex bowl. Adds salt and kefir then liberally anoints it all with more olive oil. She cannot believe what a sick villain Jacobz was, can barely imagine the terror experienced by those poor women on-board.

When she hears about the children she clutches her abdomen, leaving a floury ghost.

A slow trickle from the kettle coaxes it all to a tender ball and the comforting scent expands to fill the flat. She isn't Anatolian, but to Salima the buttery beckon of frying onions is the universal fragrance of home.

"Something smells gorgeous" Jamie pads into the kitchen, opening the fridge and washing his eyes over the shelves in a glazed sort of way. He tugs at his blonde locks and stands bathed in the cold glow while she bites her lip against explaining how much he's warming the inner temperature every time he holds the door open like that.

"What's up?" He asks. "You ok?"

"Nothing. It's...really nothing. Just thinking about...her again. You know, about Maryam."

She scrapes in the garlic and roughly hacks at handfuls of spinach before throwing it into the pan where it deflates to a verdant tangle.

"Ah Maryam," he says, turning to look at her, one hand lingering on the open door. Twisting off the heat, she pushes the mixture together with a wooden spoon while he whistles tunelessly.

She frowns and claps off excess flour over the sink before pausing the podcast and cueing up the arrow about an inch to the left of the playback timeline.

Leaning past him for a heavy cylinder from the fridge door she peels back the plastic lid and prises the ring pull to crack back the sharp metal before attacking the briny depths with a fork.

The can depicts an ecstatic lamb gambolling across a Cypriot mountaintop. It reminds her of the aggressively bland wall of cheddar in the local supermarket; each factory-hewn block pedalling a rural fantasy of milking stools and bovine joy. She smiles as Jamie hungrily watches her fish out a thick, pale coin to crumble over the wilted leaves.

She turns to tackle the dough with an empty bottle, ready to be filled and fried, briefly regretting her decision in the Cypriot place to forego dill, because no matter how cheap she cannot bear wasting the enormous bunches they're sold in. Bunches that will resemble a bouquet of dead weeds after a week in the fridge.

"Oh Sal. You need to stop obsessing about her. What can you do?"

"I know, it's just... impossible. This helps. I'm just trying to do more numbing stuff that makes me mindfully mindless or whatever."

He laughs and the sound of it makes her feel like something photosynthesising. "Well, your mindlessness smells delicious."

"You know me Jamie. I can't stand the thought of overpriced service station grimness. Besides, it all needs using up." She huffs her neon fringe from her eyes and banishes a green strand from her cheek with a dusty digit. He closes the fridge without taking anything out.

"Hmm well, I don't know about that." He pouts and squints, adopting a mock-regal tone. "One will have you know that one is rather partial to a cold baked bean pasty for nine English pounds and ninety nine pence thank you very much." He winks his lazy eye and she flicks the tea towel at him. "Besides, isn't Mrs M flat-sitting for us? Pretty sure we'll come home to a packed fridge."

"True, true. So what else do I need? Will my trainers be ok?" She asks.

"Oh they'll be fine. How have you reached the grand old age of 35 and never been to the countryside?" He asks distractedly, eyes on the pan. "Maybe wellies if you've got them? You know we really don't have to go.

I mean if you'd rather not? Isn't that Human Rights exhibition on at the Photographer's Gallery?"

She shakes her head.

"But I've never met any of them. Anyone would think *you* were the one with Asian heritage. That you were worried about upsetting the aunties with an unmarried gora in the family. Are you embarrassed of them or something?"

He continues staring at the food and she can tell he's fighting the urge to pick.

"No! ha. Really no. Nothing like that. We just aren't that close anymore you know?"

"Are you sure that's all it is?" She looks at him, closely. "Are you ashamed of...*me*? Is that it? And yes, of course I've been to the country, we had school trips and stuff you know."

He laughs too loudly.

"It's like I've said before, they're a bit different ok? Probably not like other people you've met that's all. They're slightly … umm" he searches the spinach for the word "… isolated."

They've been together for coming up to a year now and this is the most unlike himself she's ever seen him.

All the conversations they've shared, everything from the shortcomings of the political compass to how to consume a Twix (caramel then shortbread, obviously). Their adoration of Arundhati Roy and Stewart Lee and their heartbreak over the deaths of John Peel and Rik Mayall. They've talked long into the night about their hatred of the rich and their mistrust of the weather, the air and the water.

They've nicked one billboard poster, been to four gigs and three protest marches together. Jumped the fence at two music festivals and done a runner from a Michelin starred restaurant that made them feel like actual scum for daring to carry a Salvation Army bag. They've given a four fingered salute (two each) to the awfulness in the world and are still relishing their languid, steady rebellion towards one another. But this is something he refuses to be drawn on. Every time she casually mentions or asks about his family, he clams up.

Of course she and Amy have scoured the net, but astonishingly, bizarrely among all the many, many Paynes in the UK, there's no trace of them anywhere online. It's as though they don't exist.

If they hadn't both been reeling from the parallel life lines on the test she'd taken a fortnight ago, she wonders if they'd even be bothering with this visit.

She swats his fingers from the pan and he grins impishly, before pulling her into his arms. She waits, wondering how quickly the subject change will come this time.

"I love you, you crazy spinach lady" he whispers into her dusty hair, before kissing away the flour smudges from her cheeks.

"I love you too you dufus."

It's difficult to imagine ever failing to find fascination in those eyes. Her favourite, the left one is a lazy, gold-flecked emerald. The other can flicker from stormy blue to gunmetal like something from a New Order song, depending on the time of day, on the position of the sun.

* * *

"So, do I get to eat any before we road test it?" He asks through a quickly crammed mouthful taken before she can protest. When she turns back to the podcast and the unstuffed gozleme, the meditative rhythm has evaporated and she finds it impossible to focus on the words.

Instead, she silently fills and fries the first flatbread, recalling that evening at the Beacon, when her aunts had smothered his nerves with boisterous affection. How nourished she'd felt watching him properly belly laugh with her mum.

"Oshonko dhonnabad. Thank you Mrs Farooqi." He'd stammered, extending his hand and bowing slightly.

"Oh, please call me Nilofer." She'd grinned, eyes sparkling with mirth and gone in for a bear hug instead.

How about Scouting for Girls? 'Bellends flogging a novelty single from the back of a comedy bus.' Busted? 'Those gurning idiots really twist my melon.' Or Blur? 'End of the pier mockney fools.' Maybe his opinion on Coldplay might have clocked up a couple more column inches? 'Wankers.' I met Chris Martin backstage at the Brits in 2018. He was dressed like some art student's final year project, but he most definitely was not a wanker. Actually out of everyone I've met in the industry the only person deserving of that moniker was Jake. That said, the man could shift tickets: it's what snark and a well-timed Twitter beef could do. The *4/4* tour sold out in an hour, tickets snapped up by people who – according to the *NME* – 'actively disliked music' (the *NME* didn't like us much either). That was fine: they weren't the ones laughing all the way to the bank (neither we were as it turned out).

The fact that Jake had lit the blue touch paper but had forgotten to stand back was never going to end well.

I Am Kelso, Destroyer of Worlds

The *4/4* tour was a monster: logistically, financially, physically, emotionally. We had four forty foot artics loaded with five tons of gear and a stage set designed and constructed at huge expense by 59 Productions. Our crew was thirty strong and boasted a masseur and on-call pharmacist (i.e., Doctor Demetrius, the band's procurer of all things illicit). We all had our own backstage riders: Jake's listed twelve bottles of Cristal, three iced caramel lattes from Starbucks and absolutely no bananas (*"Seriously, this is a NO BANANA tour"*). He even demanded a separate dressing room that no other band member was allowed into just in case someone "harshed his mellow". The bullshit quotient was off the scale.

The first night of the tour was at the Brighton Centre, a soulless concrete outhouse on the seafront used for party political conferences and James Blunt concerts. The gig was uneventful, demoralising almost. I'd never really like playing those conference centre places: Lament's music worked best in small, sweaty clubs, venues we hadn't played in years. The *4/4* tour visited every atmosphere-free enormodome in the UK where Jake would be the focal point, the other three members of Lament lurking behind him in the non-spotlit shadows. We'd front loaded the set with songs from the new album, which didn't go down as well as the songs from *S/T* which were met with weirdly ironic cheers as if everyone had realised that *4/4* was indeed the shit sandwich everyone was saying it was. Jake was not happy. Backstage he harangued us about how the record's disappointing reception had been down to Marziale, Nick and me for not coming up with enough "arse-kicking tunes". Had Jake said the same five years before Nick would've decked him. Such as it was we just stood there and took it in the knowledge that without Jake there was no band. For the first time I understood that what we were doing was a job: we were employees. We had roles, responsibilities, schedules to adhere to, meetings to attend. No wonder we never had time to polish a second album that ended up sounding a bit turd-like. Above all else we had to put up with a workmate who we couldn't jettison as there'd be no-one out front to shine the big fucking spotlight on.

It was the first night of the tour and the wheels were coming off already.

That night I went to bed sober and alone in a mid-priced chain hotel, fearful that one half-decent album and its shonky follow-up was all we had in us. Perhaps the critics were right: Lament were circling the wagons round a large pile of average. Jake of course wasn't bothered about such things. After a series of pre-tour strops he'd secured a suite at the Grand, a crenulated Victorian pile next door to the Brighton Centre where I suspected breakfast would be presented to him on a gold platter with a couple of genuflections thrown in for good measure. I wished I was sleeping on a fan's sofa like we used to before *S/T* blew up. The fun, the excitement, the sheer, breakneck stupidity: all that had gone. Being in a successful band was a ball ache of a job just like any other.

The next morning our outsized tour bus idled outside the Grand. Jake was late; he always was. Forty minutes later he stomped on board in a foul mood: tetchy, hungover. That wasn't unusual. What was unusual was that there was a small, bloody dent in the side of his forehead that was just starting to bruise. Nobody said a word. Jake had developed a reputation for throwing his toys around at the smallest provocation. Perhaps one had bounced off something and hit him on the head. He'd probably deserved it.

The drive to Brixton was dull. Marziale and Nick played rummy with Demetrius (along for the ride as ever) for wraps of coke whilst Jake slept with his Lament hoodie pulled down over his eyes, comatose until we pulled up at the back of the Academy. We were playing three sold out nights before gigs in Birmingham, Manchester, Edinburgh and Dublin. A sojourn in Europe was next, then on to the US.

We'd toured the States before in a chaotic blaze of drugs, idiocy and abandon. Freed from Jake's studio-based hectoring I'd had the time of my life. In comparison that night I played the Brighton gig from the murk at the back of the stage whilst Jake preened his way through a set of songs I'd lost all interest in. We sounded slick, professional, over-rehearsed: in other words, we were boring. It occurred to me that this was now my life, and it was ending one uneventful gig at a time.

Four months later a post appeared on Instagram under the account ellalou2:

I met Jake Kelso on 5th May 2019. I loved Lament. Their music has helped me through some difficult times. Seeing them live was amazing and meeting Jake afterwards was exciting and a little intimidating but he was charming and funny and did his best to put me at ease. He had a suite at the Grand. We drank Champagne until we were both REALLY drunk. We ended up sleeping on the same bed. I remember him kissing me. I must've blacked out as the next thing I remember was that Jake was on top of me, inside me. I couldn't move as he'd pinned my arms to the bed. I was too shocked to do anything as I was too embarrassed, too humiliated, too frightened.

I've struggled about coming forward with this as my memory of that evening is hazy. But the one thing I do know about what happened was that I was RAPED. And my rapist's name is JAKE KELSO.

SARAH TANBURN

Born of Courage

Synopsis

A young Black woman, Calliste, becomes a naval seaman during the Napoleonic Wars. She survives storms, battles, wrecks and enslavement to win her beloved, gain a ship and make her own search for liberty.

Taken from St Lucia to English imprisonment during the Revolutionary war and mistaken for a boy, she loves the voyage; after her mother dies in childbirth during the passage, the seven-year-old girl vows to stay William Brown. By 1803 she is free and disguised, but alone; the revolution has deserted her with Napoleon's reimposition of slavery. She joins the British Royal Navy. Blockading Haiti, she meets Black captain John Perkins. He sends her to London to learn spy-craft, where she falls in love with Ruthie; they build a secret network together to collect information both to defeat Napoleon and end slavery. Their love and the project continue when Perkins takes William to Jamaica.

Ruthie wants children and marries in 1807. Heartbroken, William resumes espionage in the Caribbean and is nearly killed in battle. Shipwrecked on Guadeloupe, William is enslaved and brutalised before she escapes, joining the Maroons fighting for freedom. She finds new purpose and discovers the martyred revolutionary, Louis Delgrès, was her father. Re-joining the Navy in 1810, she nurtures the vision of a peaceful, equal state she calls Suffisance.

William gives Ruthie poison to murder her tyrannical husband but returns to sea until Perkins dies, when Jamaican authorities suspect William's sex. In 1814 she reunites with Ruthie in London. After Waterloo, William uses a newspaper interview to pressure the Admiralty to give her a ship. Ruthie is imprisoned by her father who is horrified at the revelations; she escapes just in time to join William. With their dedicated crew they sail west in search of liberty.

BORN OF COURAGE

HMS Ganges, *mid-Atlantic, August 1796*

Maman was still screaming and the baby punched against her skin. Mr Read believed my brother would be born in the night and we had rigged up a flat sheet between two cannon on the gundeck, pulled taut to make a bed for her. Sawdust was spread thick beneath.

Shadows surrounded me, dark shapes swelling and shrinking, and faces gleaming with sweat framed by lank hair. Red lips shone and vanished. An eye glistened, unshed tears offering a momentary reflection before blinking out, as if fear could be washed away by the waves. *Ganges* lurched and pitched in the swell left over from the storm. The crew had battened down the hatches over our heads, and our only illumination was three feeble candles inside glass chimneys hung above us, swinging with the sea.

The sheet was black and stiff with congealed blood. Even the ropes holding it in place were stained. I knelt by Maman's head, my hand on her elbow. I was cold clear through but dared not move. Oncle Louis stood behind me, his head bowed, his eyes sunk deep beneath his forehead. Maman would glance from me to him and back again, and smile until another spasm clenched her belly and she wailed. She held Oncle Louis' hand and once I heard his finger-bones grate, but he made no sign.

Madame Piemont, wife to our Général, was helping Mr Read while Tante Charlotte knelt the other side of the sheet. She watched Maman's face, murmured to her. I didn't hear what she said, but sometimes Maman would gaze at her like an animal mystified by pain.

'Yemaya. Marie. Makandal,' I begged all the powers I'd ever heard of to spare her for even I, a child and ignorant, could see death in the shifting shadows, in the weakness of her moans, in the surgeon's grim stance. I had been Calliste, running free in our hidden village. Suddenly I was become William, a prisoner of war surrounded by whey-faced Europeans. I loved the ocean and the life of the ship even before St Lucia dropped out of sight, but now catastrophe lurked among the cannon.

'Sigwe. My Sigwe.' Her voice was light against my ear. Only I would hear the name she had called me as a baby, my secret name.

'Sigwe, ma petite. Revolutionaries do not weep.'

I put my forehead on her shoulder.

'La liberté est née du courage. Live free, child.'

Her head rested against mine, a moment's contact before she fell back, gasping.

'Oui, Maman,' I whispered.

Oncle Louis took me in his arms. Maman lay akimbo. Her skin was dark against the brown blood and the last white corner of the sheet flickered in the lamplight. Mr Read had some steel implement in his hand. A blade. He put it in the flame and it burned red hot. Oncle Louis pulled my head against his shoulder. Maman screamed and his arms were so tight around me I couldn't breathe, my nose full of his thick jacket which smelt of gunpowder.

She shrieked again, louder this time, and tailed off to a sob.

Silence never falls on a warship. Timbers creak, water crashes against the hull, pipes and bells whistle orders and men's feet pound in answer. In that moment, her whimpers froze the sea and the ship balanced on its crest. The crew held their breath. We were a tableau, the crowd of us around the guns, the sawdust mopping up the blood, the tiny bundle in Tante Charlotte's hands, already wrapped. My sister, who never breathed.

I broke away and ran, ran up the companionways, away from the prisoners and the blood and the flashing blades and the sheet stretched taut and the body. Maman lying there. The deck hatches were ajar at last and I burst onto the foredeck. Mr Barden saw me and opened his mouth to shout, but he looked at my face and shut it again.

'Permission to climb, sir?'

'Foremast only, boy, and make yourself useful while you're there. Send Mr Fitzsimmons down and keep lookout.'

'Aye sir.' I was already on the ratlines.

The moon had set and clouds still draped the stars. From the top, the empty sea spread away, only wave-spume breaking the greys and blacks around us. Revolutionaries do not weep. The crew of a warship sheds no tears. Even prisoners may not cry. I clenched my teeth till my jaw ached and watched the foam curling under our bow. Too soon, I saw the first smear of dawn on the eastern horizon, the start of life without Maman.

I will not labour, I vowed. I will be William. Not Calliste, not Sigwe. William, who does not cry and who will never be a mother.

* * *

I wasn't there when Mr Read found them a scrap of sail cloth to wrap her in. I wasn't there when Oncle Louis retrieved his gun from the captain of the Marines and laid it at her feet. I missed the sponging of her body, the head-wrap to hold her jaw closed, the swaddling of the baby tight to her chest in the circle of her arms.

I was glaring at the horizon, infinitely far in the early morning light, wishing for a sail, a school of dolphins, even a cloud to scatter my thoughts. My eyes were dried by the glare and I could hardly blink, even when one of the boys clambered into the crow's nest beside me.

'You're wanted on deck,' he said, pointing down.

A pale bag of cloth lay at the top of the companionway. The rest of them emerged on deck, hands washed, clothes showing no speck of blood. Their hair was dampened into place. No sign of the carnage below.

The bag had a line of stitching from one end to the other. I thought I recognised Madame Piemont's careful hand in the work.

'Go,' said the boy again.

I slid into place behind Oncle Louis as the cadre moved together towards the gunwale. He held one corner, with Général Marinier, Monsieur Pedre and Capitaine Lambert at the others. An honour guard. He saw me arrive and nodded, his lips tight shut. Some of the hammocks normally stacked atop the gunwale had been removed and piled on the deck. The netting had been slackened off. The bulwark around the deck still seemed high to me, but it came only to the men's waists as they lifted the bag. I reached out and touched it, just once. It felt cold and lumpy. Nothing to do with Maman.

I could not see her hit the water. There was one splash breaking the slap of the waves against the hull, no more. The adults around me bowed their heads.

'Adieu Françoise, notre soeur dans la révolution,' said the Général.

'Adieu Francine, beloved child,' added his wife, warming me a little with my sister's name.

I heard a snigger and a whisper from behind us. 'Better than she deserved. A bag and all. The sharks will be disappointed.'

I stiffened and tried to twist towards the voice, but Oncle Louis' hand on my shoulder held me rigid. His eyes glistened like the ocean at dawn, too bright to look upon without pain.

'Adieu ma chérie,' he said. 'You were worthy of every honour.'

We turned as one, the cohort who had boarded *Ganges* some four weeks ago, and walked back across the deck. This time, the men stood aside, myself among them, and let the women precede us down into the dark, stinking prison-deck.

* * *

We had marched aboard *Ganges* on the twelfth day of Prairial, Year Four of the Revolution. The last day of May in the year of our lord 1796, as the British styled it. St Lucia had fallen, but we were revolutionaries proud to wear the tricoleur badge and only defeated by bigger, better-armed forces when France herself was encircled by enemies. From inside Fort Charlotte, we had claimed our right as free citizens of France to be treated as prisoners of war. These white men, the Jack flying over their heads, had agreed.

Maman held my hand and I matched her pace as best I could. We followed Oncle Louis and the others onto the deck where the officers welcomed Général Marinier with respect. I felt Maman's pride at the sight of white men greeting him as an equal, even as prisoners. We were not, we had never been, slaves.

One of the crew mistook me for a boy. Général Marinier seized the moment, explaining later to Maman and me that he needed sharp-witted eyes and ears about the ship, that the Revolution needed us to learn all we could about the ways of the British.

'Learn English,' he commanded me. 'Learn all you can about the Navy's ways.'

I had not expected to fall in love while I spied.

The harbour stank. Our deck reeked, hundreds of us crammed into a dark, airless hold beneath the gundeck. Crowded, insanitary and poorly furnished, a space from which there was little escape, especially for the women. Rats sneaked about and ran over our faces at night, even after we had laid out herbs and I had befriended one of the ship's cats to hunt.

It was the ship herself, *Ganges*, and the life aboard her I loved. She smelt of wood and fire and salt. I could put my face to the massive planks of her hull and inhale tar and gunpowder, and the distant memory of every wave that had risen around her in all the years since the skeleton ribs had been curved into shape.

The quiet village I had known all my life became a dream. The fast-flowing streams cooling the hot boulders where we sat dangling our feet. Greenwashed shade under the forest, alive with butterflies and squawking jacquots all around us. Maman's voice calling me home. All of it faded in the harsh light of the anchorage crowded with canoes and ships and energetic people readying for sea. Bird song and stream whisper could not compete with the clamour of this strange life, with the glamour of a ship of the line.

Everyone aboard had a job, tasks to be done now, right this moment or you'd feel the rope's end. Every day, a dozen grown men scrubbed the deck on their hands and knees. Others, dressed in hot blue jackets, shouted numbers to and fro' with youngsters in canoes. By some alchemy, agreement was reached and barrels would sway aboard on lines hauled by sweating sailors, or enormous nets of fruit, especially lemons. Haunches of ham encrusted with salt were delivered, to be lowered carefully into the coolest hold where the cook shut them in a metal cabinet as secure as the copper-lined armoury.

'Rats love that bacon even more than gunpowder,' I heard a red-coated Marine grumble.

English came fast, as it must when the choice is silence. The words blew my cheeks and lips apart, messy after the precision of the French demanded by Oncle Louis and the liquid Creole I spoke with Maman. The vowels were the wrong shape, adjectives awry.

'A ship is always she. Everyone knows that,' one of the boys said. I could not reply, *not in my tongue*. Rather, I stored away this quirk. In all the brutal it-ness of English, this extraordinary new world was, like me, female underneath it all.

At the very beginning, I was forbidden to try the masts. A frightening white man in a blue jacket with gold at the shoulders told me to 'stay on deck'. Young Mick, one of the cabin boys, saw me watching the others skylarking high above just a couple of days later. He persuaded the mate to let him show me how to climb.

I put my hand on the taut rope of the foremast port shroud and felt it shiver, warm and hairy like a favourite dog. I stroked it before placing my other hand above the first and swinging myself up to stand on the bulwark. Mick was standing in the ratlines above my head.

'Hand over hand,' he said. 'Just remember always keep one hand tight to the lines.'

I lifted a bare foot to the lathes serving as rungs in the lower parts of the climb. The sun-softened wood was comforting as I glimpsed the filthy water around us. I could not swim. The other foot, a hand at a time, and in seconds I was climbing. The vertical shrouds pinched together, rope replaced the lathes, the deck shrank away. I reached the top, the first platform, from which Marines might shoot the enemy or an extra lookout stationed at need. Its protective walls spread above me like a fan. A gap allowed access by the mast, but I already knew this was the 'lubber's hole', never to be used by any sailor.

Mick's face peered over the edge at me. 'That's it. Hold here.'

I tilted backwards, my skull suddenly vulnerable to the long fall as I looked up at the tangle of wood, ropes, canvas, blocks and string all incomprehensible from this angle. I swallowed and thought about my next move. Up or down, both seemed unlikely in that moment.

Mick's voice was clear and calm. 'Right hand here. Left, there. Pull up now.'

I stood upright on the platform, half the mast still above me. Mick slapped me on the back.

'You're a natural. Ready to keep going?'

I nodded, exhilaration stripping all English from my tongue.

The next stage took me closer to the yards, the great beams running port to starboard, the sails neatly tied up against them while we tarried at anchor. There were six to each mast and I already knew their names, chanting them like a spell: course, lower fore, upper fore, lower top-gallant, and upper top-gallant, and finally the royal. At the upper top-gallant, four sails up from the deck, one of the bosun's mates was changing a block, a line held between his teeth.

'Can I help?'

'Hold this,' he slurred. I picked the damp line from his mouth and watched as he removed the worn block, storing it in a bag at his waist.

'Mustn't drop it,' he said. 'You could kill someone, it hit them on the head.'

I glanced down. It was a long fall.

He took the thin rope from me.

'Thanks, lad.'

I clambered on, feeling I had played a valuable role in this enormous, beautiful world of wood and men. Maybe that strong new block will save us all one day, I thought.

The crow's nest, a few feet below the mast cap, was a platform big enough for Mick and me to stand and gaze away from the land, outwards at the open sea. The blue indentation of the horizon met the white glare of the sky, a promise without limits.

Biographies

Judge's Biography

Ross Raisin is the author of four novels: *A Hunger* (2022), *A Natural* (2017), *Waterline* (2011) and *God's Own Country* (2008). His work has won and been shortlisted for over ten literary awards. He won the Sunday *Times* Young Writer of the Year award in 2009, and in 2013 was named on Granta's once a decade Best of Young British Novelists list. In 2018 he was awarded a Fellowship by the Royal Society of Literature. Find more on Ross, his books and teaching here: www.rossraisin.com

Author Biographies

Laura Allsop is a writer and editor with a specialism in art and culture. She has written on art and film for titles including *The Guardian, Time Out, AnOther Magazine*, *ArtReview* and *Frieze*, among many others, and edited books about fashion, architecture and interiors, and travel for Berlin publishers, gestalten. Laura completed an MA in Creative Writing from Birkbeck, University of London, in 2010 and has a BA in English Literature from the University of Cambridge. She lives in London with her family; between 2019 and 2020 she lived in Vancouver, British Columbia.

Alex Cassidy is a sports historian and author. His first book, *American Football's Forgotten Kings*, was a non-fiction exploration into the professional gridiron team that existed in London in the 1990s, and was published in 2015. He has two other self-published works, *Sunshine* and *Cracks of the Puzzle* which tackle the subject of mental health and concussions in sport. He spends his time between Brittany and London. As well as writing he runs regularly, reads a lot, and dabbles in other ad hoc creative projects. You can follow him at @alexcass91 on X or at www.alexcassidy.com.

Elizabeth Champion grew up in Lincolnshire and lives in London. She studied Modern History at Oxford and then joined the civil service. Elizabeth began writing when her children were small. She started out with children's stories before diversifying into writing for grown-ups. Her writing for children has been longlisted and shortlisted in competitions including the Greenhouse Funny Prize and the Searchlight Awards. Her debut novel for adults, *The Hardest Word,* explores generational shifts in attitudes to consent. It was longlisted in the 2023 Mslexia Adult Novel Competition. Elizabeth is currently completing an MA in Creative Writing at Bath Spa University.

Charlotte Cole is a writer of horror and surrealist fiction. She writes on female identity, sexuality, and relationships between women. Originally starting her career in fashion editorial, Charlotte then moved into digital retail, before landing in the non-profit arts sector. She is currently completing an MA in Creative and Life Writing at Goldsmiths and works at Chisenhale Gallery in East London. *Babygirl* is Charlotte's first novel. Instagram: @cjlcole, Substack: @Ad Infinitum

Jennifer Coles worked in film before training as a psychotherapist. In both careers, she has followed her interest in relationships and how, in spite of our best efforts, we can mess them up. She interrogates the same theme in her writing, following fictional characters down the strange paths they create for themselves. *Flotsam* was conceived in lockdown, when time and space collapsed and the world felt small. She is now living in Norwich and working on new stories, *Wildfire* and *Larks*.

Anna Dempsey is a writer and teacher from Florida, now living in London. She's working on a PhD in Creative Writing and Grieving at Bath Spa University and Bristol University. Anna won the 2019 Costa Short Story Award and was long-listed for the Curtis Brown Discoveries Prize. She teaches creative writing with The Writing Set and co-runs Path2Pen, a creative hiking group she started with her best friend. Website: annadempsey.me

Amy Elkheart is a writer, developmental editor and workshop facilitator from Belfast who holds a Creative Writing MA from University of Limerick. *Manhattan Star* received support from the Arts Council of Northern Ireland and was mostly written at a windowsill with a glass of wine during a Centre Culturel Irlandais residency. As a Society of Authors Associate Member, Amy's writing has also received support from the Irish Writers Centre, the Prince's Trust, the John Hewitt Society and Writers' HQ, of which they were awarded Gold Star sponsorship.

E. H. Ewart is an Irish sculptor who has lived and worked largely in New York City and Ghent, Belgium. She is a graduate of the Ontario College of Art, Toronto, and her many bodies of work have been exhibited in museums in North America and Europe. Her sculpture finally developed into "sign structures", which offered up the possibility of what was to become her first novel, *The Pope is Dead*. She lives with her husband in Waterloo, Ontario, where she is working on her second novel.

Marie Gethins work features in *Winter Papers*, Bristol Short Story Prize, *Australian Book Review*, NFFD Anthologies, *Fictive Dream*, Bath Short Story Prize, *Litro*, *REED* and others. Awarded BA's in English Literature and Dramatic Art/Dance from U.C. Berkeley, an MSt in Creative Writing from the University of Oxford and a PhD in Creative Writing from the University of Limerick. She received a Frank O'Connor Bursary, a Banff Center for Arts and Creativity residency and is a Hawthornden Fellow. Selected for BIFFY50, Best Microfictions, Best Small Fictions, she's the flash fiction editor for *Banshee*, co-edits for *Splonk*, and lives in Cork, Ireland.

Alison Theresa Gibson grew up in Canberra, the illusive capital of Australia, and currently lives in Birmingham, UK. She has stories published in a number of places, including *Spelk*, *Litro*, *Mechanics' Institute Review*, *Meanjin*, *Sunlight Press*, and *Every Day Fiction*. She was nominated for Best Small Fictions in 2021 and Best of the Net in 2019. She completed her MA in Creative Writing at University of Birmingham in 2021. *Bound in Shallows* is a work in progress, and her fifth (all unpublished!) novel. Find her @byAlisonTheresa and alisontheresa.com

Chris Hancock is a passionate linguist who spent a number of years living in St Petersburg, Russia, where the idea for his debut novel – a queer upmarket thriller – was born. Chris trained as an actor at Bristol Old Vic Theatre School and performed at venues such as Sheffield Crucible and Hull Truck. He subsequently worked in theatre production and toured the globe with a magic and illusion show, *Impossible*. As a writer, he is a graduate of the Curtis Brown Write Your Novel course and his short stories have previously been shortlisted for the Bridport Prize in 2021.

Mónica Ibarra Parle grew up shuttling between the bayous of southeast Texas and her grandparents' house in Ciudad Juárez, Chihuahua. She has three novels in progress (two lit novels and a YA) and won the 2022 Mslexia Short Story Competition. Her work has also been short-listed for the 2021 Bridport Prize Peggy Chapman First Writing Award, the 2021 Wasafiri Queen Mary Prize, and highly commended in Faber's 2018 Fab Prize. She now lives in London and is the Co-Executive Director of Forward Arts Foundation (the Forward Prizes and National Poetry Day) and Associate Director of El Nuevo Sol British Latinx writers.

Susan Kemp is a writer from Scotland who has been a little distracted by a career in film and film education. She won a highly commended for a short story at school many decades ago, and which acknowledgment sparked the fire. She was shortlisted for the Richard & Judy Publishing Competition and later for the Sceptre Prize in 2008. She was shortlisted for the Bridport Short Story competition in 2018. She has an Mlitt in Creative Writing from Glasgow University and is currently employed as a Senior Lecturer at the University of Edinburgh. *Wildish* is her first novel. Susan-Kemp.com

Zoe McCann lives in Belfast and has a chequered career history that doesn't lend itself well to biographies. She's been a support worker, a singer and an English tutor, and she shows no signs of alighting on a job she can bear to stay in for longer than six months. She has an MPhil in English and she's grateful that no one really knows what that means. She recently self-published her debut novel, *The Drink Shrink*, and she continues to dream that one day she might be able to retire from the so-called real world altogether. @zomccann on Instagram.

Sam McNeilly grew up in Portsmouth, and currently spends his time between Pakistan, Ireland, and the UAE. He plans a permanent return to the UK soon. Last year, Sam completed a PhD in Literature at the University of Surrey, where he also lectured in the English department. Now working as a researcher and consultant, he began writing his first novel, *Why I Shot the Elephant*, while living in Lahore with his wife, Naseeba.

Terri Mullholland is a writer, researcher, and teacher who grew up in the West Country and now lives in London. She has a PhD from the University of Oxford, where she has taught English Literature and Critical Theory. Her writing has appeared in various journals and anthologies, including *Ellipsis*, *Litro*, and *Mercurious*. She was awarded third prize in the Edinburgh Award for Flash Fiction 2024. Her pamphlet of hybrid pieces *Weather / Patterns* was published by intergraphia books. When not writing she can be found curled up with a cat and a good book. Find her at: https://www.terrimullholland.com/ Instagram @terri_mullholland

Kate Packman left Lincolnshire for London life in 2001 but a love of reading pushed her towards an English degree, librarianship and eventually teaching. She writes fiction, including children's literature, and non-fiction articles from her home in Bedfordshire. Her novel, *You Can See the End of the World From Here,* evolved during her creative writing MA (Birkbeck

College, University of London). Kate chaired @AmpLiterary (2017-2022) and hosts @AmpthillBeerandBooks, a pub-based book club. She likes to experiment with her use of time and the ever-changing identities of her characters in her work. Find her on X @PackmanKate

Rejina Sabur-Cross is a British-Bangladeshi from a horrible London suburb. Her morbid fascination with the rise of the Far Right inspired this novel. She's worked in Japan, for the late Sir John Peel and sat on the Rich Mix board. She's also been a television researcher, a food writer (*The Guardian*, BBC Good Food, C4), featured in Sainsbury's food waste campaign and narrated audio tours. She helped launch Farm:Shop Dalston with eco-arts collective Something & Son. One of two to be approached by an agent on the Creative Writing Programme at New Writing South, she lives in Brighton.

Christopher Smith, originally from Salisbury but now residing in the lively city of Brighton, holds an MA in Narrative Illustration and Editorial Design from the University of Brighton. Over the past twenty years, he has built a career in commercial management and dispute resolution. In his leisure time Christopher collects records, books and dogs. He previously played bass in a noise rock band and has recently made the decision to set aside attempts at learning the cello. Twitter: @chip_smith

Sarah Tanburn is a writer living in South Wales. She spent years afloat and is fascinated by the lives of women at sea under sail. Her short stories, essays, memoirs and reviews have appeared online and in print. Her collection of magical realist novellas, *Children of the Land* came out in 2023. *Born of Courage* is part of her PhD at Swansea University. It is the first of two books set in the North Atlantic at the start of the nineteenth century, featuring Black sailor and mistress of disguise, William Brown. X: @workthewind